Beneath An Ivy Moon

By

Ellen Dugan

Beneath An Ivy Moon
Copyright @ Ellen Dugan 2016
Edited by Katherine Pace
Cover art designed by Kyle Hallemeier
Cover image: fotolia
"Legacy of Magick" logo designed by Kyle Hallemeier
Copy Editing and Formatting by Libris in CAPS

This is a work of fiction. Names, characters, businesses, organizations, places, events and incidents either are the product of the author's imagination or are used fictitiously. Any resemblance to actual persons, living or dead, events, or locales is entirely coincidental.

Excerpt of: Under The Holly Moon
Copyright © Ellen Dugan 2016
Edited by Katherine Pace
Copy Editing and Formatting by Libris in CAPS

Other titles in the Legacy of Magick Series
by Ellen Dugan

Legacy of Magick, Book #1

Secret of the Rose, Book #2

Message of the Crow, Book #3

Coming in 2016

Under the Holly Moon, Book #5

ACKNOWLEDGMENTS

Thanks to the friends, family, and fans who have enthusiastically supported me, and this series.

A few words of appreciation to my lovely research assistant, Janet.

A very special thank you to my Beta Readers: Shawna and Erin.

To my editor Katherine, who is always a pleasure to work with; and to Kyle for such gorgeous cover art for the novels.

Creeping where no life is seen,

A rare old plant is the ivy green.

-Charles Dickens

CHAPTER ONE

I was minding my own business in the University library when I got my first inkling that something was wrong. As a rush of sensation rolled over me, my belly tightened. I sat up straight in my chair, all my spidey senses on alert. It was nothing I could physically see, hear, or touch with my own two hands... but I *felt* it in my gut, nonetheless. A foreboding feeling that pushed me to move. To do something, to scan my own surroundings for danger, and to check on my family and friends... Something was coming, and everything would change.

As the premonition rolled over me I shivered, tugging my short, black jacket closer around me. Waiting to see if I got a 'hit' in my solar plexus, I silently ran down a mental list of the names of my nearest and dearest: *Great Aunt Faye, Bran, Lexie, Morgan, Autumn, Rene, Marie, Cypress, Holly...* I was searching for a sort of 'energetic tweak' as my cousin Autumn called it, something that would let me know where to pinpoint my focus.

And there it was— *Holly*. I got the energetic hit on my absent twin sister. I sighed, pushed my laptop away from me, and sat back to think. Things had been pretty quiet (magickally speaking) in William's Ford... ever since the big magickal showdown between the Drake family and mine.

The crazy, evil practitioner who had caused so many problems was dead and buried, and the Blood Moon Grimoire was safely under the protection of the Proctor family— Lexie's family. I was starting my Junior year at University, and Cypress Rousseau and I were still roommates and still witchy BFFs.

So my life as a college student was pretty good, but I'd be lying if I said there wasn't a big emotional vacancy in my world. And her name was Holly. My twin sister Holly had moved away, choosing to go to a college clear across the state. Besides the occasional text, email or phone call— that I always instigated— I rarely heard from her.

Losing our mother during the quest for the Grimoire had been horrible. I missed her actively every day. For a long time I didn't think anything would ever be worse than losing my Mom. But circumstances had proven me wrong, because having my sister, *my twin* shut me out, made me feel like a part of me was physically missing. Holly had been my other magickal half. We had practiced together since we were little, our spells working together in a sort of two part harmony— I suppose. Having that part of my life taken away left me floundering. Not that she cared.

I will never understand Holly's choice to turn away from the Craft. And I couldn't even imagine how she made it through every day without the support of the family. I hoped she was happy in her new life, pretending to be a mundane, while she studied Art History at her college in Kansas City while I struggled to go forward on my own. Magick aside, I honestly missed seeing and talking to her every day, however there were *other* ways, *magickal ways*, of keeping in touch with my fraternal twin. And as of yet, she hadn't been able to block me out.

I checked around, making sure that I was unobserved in the little glass-walled study room I had rented. All I saw was my own reflection against the glass walls. I lifted a hand to my shorter hair. *Yeah, the cut had been a good choice.* The subtle touch of a few caramel highlights stood out against my brown hair and it drew attention to my new stacked bob. It was a fun and kicky haircut— just brushing my shoulders, and I was happy with it.

Sometimes I missed the crazy purple and blue I used to dye my hair back in the day, but I did not miss the fried, damaged ends. Now my hair was healthy and shiny, and the natural brown suited me better. Plus it, helped to make my green eyes more noticeable.

I dropped my hand, smirking at myself for primping. I checked again to see if anyone was paying attention to me. No one was, and the coast was clear. I propped my feet up on the desk, smoothing my short black dress with white skulls all over it, down over my thighs. *Don't want to accidentally flash the campus boys, Ivy.* I reminded myself.

I tipped back in my chair, shut my eyes and reached out energetically to my twin. I found the psychic bond we still shared, and visualized that unbreakable energetic silver cord that connected me to her. I gave it a good hard yank on the astral plane. Ha! That would get her attention. *Holly, what's up, sis?* I called out to her on the astral.

I felt an answering tug at my solar plexus. *I'm studying Ivy. I'm fine.* Came Holly's annoyed reply.

Mentally I rolled my eyes, and I let my sister 'feel' that. *Why... do I not believe you?*

Because you like to create drama where there is none.

Hey, I sent back, a little hurt at the dismissive comment. *I had a premonition and it felt like something was wrong. I was worried about you.*

Don't be. I'm happy here.

How would I know? I asked. *I didn't even see you this summer. What with you staying with Dad... and what the hell did you do on a farm in Iowa all summer? Gather eggs? Sew a quilt?*

I did gather some eggs, now that you mention it... It seemed that Holly was chuckling. *But I do have to get back to my studies. Gotta go now.* I felt the link lessening between the two of us as Holly tried to dissolve our psychic communication.

Before I lost her I sent out: *I miss you. Love you Holly.*

Her response came back. *Love you too Ivy, stay out of trouble.* After a moment's pause she added. *Be safe.* Then, there was nothing else.

Our psychic communication over, I opened my eyes and dropped my booted feet to the floor, setting the chair back on all four legs. Taking in a deep steadying breath, I held it for a four count, blew it out slowly and reconnected my energy to the earth. I'd expected to feel better after checking in with my twin, but if anything, a stronger feeling of unease rolled over me. Concerned, I gathered up my things for the walk back across campus to my dorm.

As I left the cool of the air conditioned library I understood that whatever *it* was, it was coming from somewhere within the campus itself. I moved over to the edge of the sidewalk, squinting my eyes to use my peripheral vision to 'see'.

There. I intuitively shifted towards the west. *It was coming from that direction... it was gaining strength, and rising.* I felt my heart skip a beat, then beat faster in reaction to the discovery. I took a deep breath, blew it out slowly and visualized that I was, once again, firmly connected to the earth.

I looked over my shoulder to regard the library. It made sense that the energy had been muffled while I'd been inside. Almost as if whatever was 'out here' had been energetically barred from the library... which would be my brother Bran's doing. He'd keep the University library locked down good and tight with his magick. After all, he worked there full time. But still, I wondered about Holly's closing message. Why would Holly have told me to 'be safe'?

Well I could damn sure find out. I may be a college student but there was more to me than most folks realized. I am Ivy Bishop. The gothic-fabulous and youngest female Witch of my generation.

As the sun set, I walked quickly back to my dorm. But instead of enjoying a pretty, late August afternoon all of my physical and witchy senses were on full alert. A chill slid down my back despite the warmth of the evening. The feeling of 'wrongness' seemed to tease the edge of my awareness. I glanced over my shoulder and saw nothing. But I knew it was there, waiting and gathering strength.

Obviously the time of peace and quiet that William's Ford had been blessed with— was over.

***

I let myself in the dorm room that I shared with Cypress Rousseau and found her exactly where I expected. Her dark, thick hair was pulled back into a low ponytail away from her pretty face. Cypress pounded away at the computer keys, her head bouncing in time to the music she was listening to. She wore ripped jeans, a University t-shirt in purple and grey, and silver noise canceling headphones. Even in a jeans and t-shirt, Cypress was stunning. If she wasn't my closest friend I'd probably be resentful.

Her skin was a striking tawny color, thanks to the ethnic diversity of her ancestors. To her amusement people often assumed she was bi-racial, Hispanic, or possibly Native American. As Cypress often remarked, technically they were all correct— she was Creole. And whatever her genetic background, it was a gorgeous mixture.

To get her attention, I concentrated on her open water bottle sitting next to her. I tapped into my telekinesis and made the bottle slide over to hover at the edge of the desk. Cypress jolted as the bottle came into her line of sight. She laughed. "Ivy!"

I set my laptop down on my own desk and waved at her. "Hey there, Cy."

She tugged her headphones off and pointed at the bottle. "You're not going to make that spill on me, are you?"

I focused again and the bottle slid back to where it started from.

Cypress stood up, capped the bottle, and stretched. "Wanna go grab some supper at the commons?"

"I'm not in the mood for cafeteria food." I peeled off my jacket, laid it over my desk chair, and tossed my books towards my bed. "We could always drop by the manor and mooch a free meal."

Cypress' eyes, a unique smoky-gray color shot through with amber, sparkled. "I like that idea even better." She shut down her laptop. "Do you need to call ahead and let them know we are coming?"

"Hang on, I'll let Aunt Faye know." I focused my mind on my great aunt. And I *knew*. I had the impression of her lifting her head, nodding, and pulling out more plates and silverware. I blinked, then smiled at Cypress. "We're good."

Cypress hopped up and grabbed her purse. "Let's go then."

We locked our door and headed down the steps and towards the main lobby of the building. Our dorm, Crowly Hall, had been redecorated several years ago, but the building itself dated back to 1857. The columned, brick, three story dormitory was the oldest building on campus. It boasted three cozy floors of dorm rooms for women. It was the smallest of all of the dorms, and oddly enough it was never full. While Crowly Hall maintained its historical charm, and was centrally located on campus— it was also rumored to be haunted. Hence the lack of volunteers to actually live in the dorm.

We jogged down the steps to the lobby and stopped for a moment while Cypress went through her routine of hunting for her car keys inside of her voluminous purse. A murmur of conversations came from the scattering of residents hanging out or studying in the lounge. I noted that the residence advisor, Leann, was giving a lecture on the history of the building to a half dozen new residents.

"Before it was a university," Leann said, gesturing to the portrait centered above the fireplace mantle, "Victoria Crowly was the creator of what was originally a finishing school for young ladies. In the 1850s her school became a college for women, the first west of the Mississippi River. Today, William's Ford is a full university with undergrad, Masters, and Doctorate programs." Leann paused and measured her audience. "But it all began here with this one woman in this very building, and her dream of creating a school for girls almost two hundred years ago."

Leann continued with the history and architecture of Crowly Hall itself. I tried to see the lounge through the eyes of our newest residents. Someone— probably a frustrated interior design student— had tried to redecorate our lounge in a pseudo Victorian-era style, and the current results were hit and miss. A faux-leather settee faced the fireplace. On either end of the mantle, huge, fussy silk arrangements of flowers were arranged in white ceramic vases. Fancy chairs of dark wood with their seats covered in burgundy velour fabric were arranged around a large, carved wooden table. The wine-red area rug was centered over floors stained in a deep dark brown. The room seemed out of time, and in my opinion, too prim and proper.

My gaze was pulled to the old portrait. Victoria

Crowly smiled down on the residents of the hall. To me, the dark-eyed brunette looked like she was forever keeping a secret. Maybe I was supernaturally suspicious — but despite the woman's admirable history, I still didn't like her expression. It creeped me out.

"Tell them about the ghost, Leann," I suggested, grinning when Leann scowled at me, and the new residents all gasped in unison.

"A ghost?" one girl piped up.

"Really?" someone else said.

Leann attempted to calm her group. "According to local legend, it is Victoria's ghost that is rumored to guard over the Hall. There are dozens of stories from the ridiculous to the disturbing about her ghostly visitations over the years. It's campus legend and nothing more," she stated firmly.

I shrugged off Leann's disapproval. Personally, I felt the tales of a haunting at my dorm only added to the atmosphere, but sometimes I wondered if Cy's unique blend of witchy Hoodoo combined with my magick kept Victoria's ghost at bay. So far neither Cypress nor I had seen anything, but we both had heard noises at night coming from the attic above our room. A constantly locked, empty attic.

Studying the portrait, I shrugged and told myself not to look for trouble where there was none. Truth be told, ghosts didn't scare me. I'd seen and interacted with my Grandmother's ghost back at the family manor. *Ghosts I could handle.*

While Cypress continued to search for her car keys, I noticed one of the new residents gazing up at the glass encased painting. As I watched, she took out her cell phone and snapped a picture of the old faded portrait. I nudged Cypress. "Check that out," I said, tilting my head towards the new resident. I was pretty sure her name was Jessica, and she changed angles and took another photo. *She'd never get a decent photo with a cell phone camera. She has to compensate for the glare of the glass and the lighting in the room...* I grinned at my photography geek's inner monologue.

Cypress shook her purse. She scowled when she heard her keys jingle. "I swear my keys are always disappearing in this thing."

"Try the outside pocket," I suggested, staring again at that portrait.

The house phone began to ring. Since I was the closest to the desk in the foyer, I grabbed the landline. "Crowly Hall henhouse. Which chick would you like to speak to?"

"Ivy!" Leann glared at me.

"Hang on," I said to the person on the phone. I grinned at Leann. "It's for you."

Leann scowled. "How many times do I have to tell you *not* to answer the phone like that?"

"Oh at least a dozen more," I said, as she stomped over and snatched the receiver away from me.

The girls from the group were all smiling now as they waited in the foyer. "Welcome to Crowly Hall," I said formally, and sketched a bow.

Cypress finally found her keys. Right where I told her to look, in the outside pocket. "Ah-ha!" she cried.

"You're welcome," I said to Cypress, watching Jessica as she kept trying to get a good picture. My gaze shifted from Jessica, then back to the portrait. I shivered.

Cypress finally pulled her keys out of her purse and tugged me along with her out the front doors. We walked out across the columned porch, down the steps, and to the nearby parking lot.

"So, I was wondering... have you felt anything *unusual* on campus lately?" I asked climbing into Cypress' silver VW Beetle.

"Define *unusual*." Cypress started the car. "We live in the haunted dorm— and we're both Witches."

"Point taken." I stuck my sunglasses on my nose. Still," I said. "I sensed something today. A negative energy of sorts. It started as soon as I stepped out of the library."

Cypress flipped on the A/C, glancing over at me. "You didn't pick up on it when you were *in* the library, but once you were outside?"

"Right."

Cypress pursed her lips as she thought it over. "Well it only makes sense that your brother would keep the library energetically clean." She pulled to the exit of the parking lot and stopped. "What were your first intuitive impressions? Did the energy feel sour; was it negative, or malevolent?"

I tucked my hair behind my ears. "It made my heart jump in my chest. Whatever it is— it's gaining strength, and rising."

"Rising?" Cypress repeated.

I frowned. "Yeah, *rising* was the word that popped into my mind."

"Weird choice of words." Cypress tilted her head. "Think you could follow the energetic trail?"

I nodded. "Sure, I can follow it."

"I'll drive by the library building. Let's see what you pick up with your claircognizance." Cypress turned the car and drove slowly along the main campus drive.

I shut my eyes and focused on my solar plexus and waited for that tugging sensation that would tell me I was close. Being a psychic intuitive, or more correctly a claircognizant, had its advantages. What many non-magickal folks would dismiss as a 'gut hunch'— is actually their intuition. It's a strong psychic ability, and everyone has it to some degree. But many people choose to ignore it. As a Witch, I not only accepted it, I put my psychic abilities to work.

A few moments later I felt my stomach roll over. "Got it," I said.

Cypress slowed the car to a stop. "We're at the little intersection before the library."

I opened my eyes. "Hang a right," I said.

My stomach tightened even more as Cypress turned right, and we cruised along. When we approached the campus building that housed the local history museum, my heart started to trip faster in my chest.

"Isn't this the building Autumn works in?" Cypress asked.

"Yeah, it is." I swallowed. "It's also where Julian Drake works." *Had he fallen off the wagon and was practicing dark magick again?*

"Are you okay?" Cypress reached over and gave my hand a squeeze.

I glanced over at her. I'd once had an up-close and personal encounter with Julian Drake. And even though he'd been on his best behavior for the past couple of years, I still didn't like him. "I'm fine. No worries."

Cypress pulled into the lot and parked. "Let's get out and walk around." Her face was set, and her eyes were intense.

We met at the front of the car and fell into step together. I glanced over at her, and *knew*. "You're feeling it too, aren't you?" I asked.

"Yeah, like my skin is crawling," Cypress whispered to me as we passed a group of students leaving the building.

The energetic tug was stronger as we walked around the side of the museum. We followed the path through the museum's little garden, and even thought the trees were lush and green and their leaves waved in the breeze, it was conspicuously cooler. I shuddered. "It's stronger over here."

"But what's causing it?" Cypress said.

I stopped dead in my tracks. Adjacent to the history building a large area had recently been fenced off. Bulldozers and trucks were all neatly lined up. "They must have started on the expansion of the museum. Autumn's been talking about this for months," I said, inspecting the beginnings of the project. Grass had been scraped off, and a stand of scraggly old trees had been removed. I actively wished for my camera.

As we looked over the job site there were other students also checking out the changes to the campus. Cypress nudged me. "Let's get closer." We stopped right in front of the fence. "Aww, they bulldozed all of the apple trees," she said, pointing.

I frowned at the tangle of bulldozed trees. I could see a few apples still hanging on the fallen branches. "I loved those trees," I said. "They were so old and gnarly."

"We've been snitching yellow apples from them for the past two years," Cypress sighed. "I'm going to miss that."

I tipped my head up and checked the sky. We were facing west, and the setting sun painted the clouds in a rosy hue. "West," I murmured. "Earlier I had felt pulled towards the west."

"You also said that whatever it was, that it was *rising*." Cypress curled her fingers through the tall cyclone fence as she considered it.

The hair rose off the back of my neck. "I really want to talk to Autumn, and see if she's noticed anything." I stepped back. "Let's go."

Cypress nodded, and we silently walked back to the parking lot. So now I knew where it was coming from. But I still had no idea what *it* was.

***

Cypress whipped her car across town to the manor. The tall wrought iron gates at the end of the manor's driveway swung closed behind us as she pulled in. She slammed her car door and came over to loop her arm through mine. "Let's go get dinner and see what we can find out."

"Ready for a nice quiet evening with the Bishops?" I teased, tucking my sunglasses on top of my head.

I barely got the front door of the manor opened when my little nephew Morgan came barreling towards me and Cypress.

"I—ee!" he squealed, in his toddler speak version of my name.

I caught him before he overbalanced onto his face. "Hey Morgan!" I swung him up to my hip, and pressed a loud smacking kiss to his mouth.

"Hi!" he shouted, all smiles.

"Hi cutie," Cypress ran a hand over his bright red hair.

"Cy!" Morgan puckered up his lips in her direction.

Laughing, Cypress obliged him, and I saw Bran standing in the foyer. "It's the funniest thing..." he said.

"Morgan started shouting your names about five minutes ago."

Cypress and I walked over to my brother. "Really?" I asked.

"Yeah, he kept running around the manor, like he was looking for the both of you." Still dressed in his conservative dark suit and tie, Bran rubbed a hand across his chin.

"Maybe he *saw* us coming." I shrugged.

Bran's eyes went sharp as he considered it. "Morgan's only two years old. He's a little young to be displaying any magickal abilities."

Autumn popped in from the family room. "Or maybe he takes after me, and is a Seer," she said.

Morgan snuggled his head under my chin. "My I—ee." He wrapped his little arms around me and sighed.

"Say, Ivy," Bran said to his son. "Try and say it."

Morgan pulled back to look me square in the eye. His blue eyes twinkled. "Ivy," he said slowly.

"You got it, little dude!" I gave him a hug.

Morgan squirmed and I set him down. He grinned up at his father and pointed, "Dude," he said clearly.

"Daddy," Bran corrected, while I struggled not to laugh.

Morgan pointed at Cypress. "Cy," he said clearly. He pointed at me. "Ivy," he pronounced it carefully. He stopped and grinned over at Autumn. "Tum!" He laughed and ran out of the foyer towards the back of the house.

I grinned over at my brother. "Obviously, the child is a genius."

There was a crash coming from the back of the house and Bran cringed. "An evil genius, maybe." He went to see what Morgan had gotten into.

"Hello girls." Great Aunt Faye popped her head from around the kitchen and into the family room. "I'll have dinner ready in fifteen minutes."

"Thanks," I said, and she nodded and went back into the kitchen. Knowing my great aunt's preference to be left alone when she was cooking, I didn't offer to help.

Autumn beckoned Cypress and I into the family room. "What really brings you girls by?" She dropped onto the big oversized chair, tossing her shoulder length hair behind her.

I sat on the couch, propped up my feet on the coffee table, and sighed loudly. "Maybe we wanted some home cooking?" I said.

Autumn raised an eyebrow at me. Our eyes, almost identical shades of green, locked. I felt a little pull from her mind. "Ivy," she warned me in a soft voice.

I fluttered my lashes. "Perhaps, I missed the love and comfort of my quiet little family..." My dramatic comment had Cypress rolling her eyes, and as Bran chased a happily squealing Morgan through the foyer, she snorted out a laugh.

"Don't bullshit me, Ivy," Autumn said. "I've been having weird dreams about you for the past few days."

"Did they involve Tom Hiddleston?" I joked. When

my cousin scowled at me I shrugged. "He's my newest movie star crush..."

"I'm serious," Autumn said.

I felt a much stronger tug on my mind. My temples throbbed from my cousin's psychic maneuver. "Hey! I tossed up my hands in laughing surrender. "I was going to tell you. You don't have to scan me." I laughed, rubbing my temples.

"You know how I feel about lies and secrets," Autumn said.

"Boy, what happened to the days when you weren't sure of your powers and hesitated in using them?" I teased.

"Nothing's wrong with being confident." Autumn smirked at me.

Cypress tucked her feet up and grinned at Autumn. "You're stronger now. And happy being in a relationship with my Uncle Rene. You two are good for each other, and it shows."

Autumn's face lit up. Momentarily distracted, she leaned back and beamed at the two of us. "Rene is simply one of the best men I have ever known."

Bran walked into the room with a squirming Morgan in his arms. "Hey, what about me? No props for your big brother?"

Autumn turned to him with a grin. "Did you just use the word 'props' in a sentence?"

Bran wrestled with a giggling Morgan. "I'm hip, I'll have you know."

I had a snarky comeback all ready for him, but before I could use it my sister-in-law Lexie came home from work.

Lexie let the front door shut with a slam and planted her hands on her hips. "Where's my men?" In her police uniform with her blonde hair pulled back in a neat bun, she seemed very happy to be home. *She's had a really tough day.* I suddenly knew. I frowned, imagining what a 'tough day' might actually entail for a police officer.

"Mommy!" Morgan squirmed down and ran to his mother. She scooped him up and pressed a loud kiss to his face.

I watched my brother go and kiss his wife. The three of them went upstairs together. I didn't bother to hide my smile at the picture they made.

I glanced over at Autumn, and she was holding herself very still in her chair. She shifted her gaze to mine. "Lexie's okay," she said, addressing my thoughts without me having to ask— out loud.

Cypress leaned forward. "Is something wrong?" she asked us.

Autumn blew out a slow controlled breath. "I picked up on a few images when she walked in the manor. Domestic dispute call." Autumn shook her head sadly. "It was a bad one, because she's not shaking it off."

"There's times when I wish I could see pictures the way you do..." I said to my cousin. "Then I change my mind and I decide that I really don't want to be clairvoyant," I admitted. "*Knowing* is enough for me."

"Clairvoyance means clear-seeing and claircognizance is clear-knowing," Autumn pointed out. "They are simply different facets of our psychic abilities. Ivy, I know that you dream of the past and the future as well."

"And your point is?" I said.

"My point is, that if you want to get technical, a precognitive or postcognitive dreamer *is* using a type of clairvoyance."

I made a face. "I never thought about it that way."

"But you didn't come to the manor to talk about psychic ability." Autumn crossed her arms. "So one of you tell me why you're really here."

CHAPTER TWO

"We'd like to get your opinion on something," I said.

"Okay." Autumn shifted forward.

I glanced at Cypress, she made a 'go ahead' motion with her hands.

"Have you detected any type of sour energy or negative vibes since they started working on the expansion of the museum on campus?" I asked.

"No," Autumn said, "but I haven't been on campus in the past few days."

"I felt this negative energy when I left the library today, and I knew something, somewhere was off." I quickly explained how Cypress and I had followed the energetic trail and where it had led us.

Autumn blinked at me. "So they've started construction? They've broken ground on the expansion for the museum?"

Cypress shivered. "Broken ground. Those words sound a little creepy all of the sudden."

"Are you channeling your Native American

heritage?" I asked Cypress.

"Maybe." Cypress narrowed her eyes as she thought about her reaction. "According to Marie, there is a little in our family tree."

"Regardless, they do have to excavate to begin to lay the foundation for the new building..." Autumn trailed off. As if she realized something, her eyes jumped to mine.

"What?" I asked her

"*Foundation*," she said with emphasis. "That word is important."

"Something is coming," I heard myself say. "I know it... and it's rising from beneath." I shook my head to clear it, and saw that both Autumn and Cypress were staring at me.

"*Rising from beneath*. That's an interesting choice of words," Autumn said.

Cypress nodded. "That's exactly what I said earlier."

"Now I'm starting to understand why I've been having the same recurring dream for the past few nights." Autumn tapped a finger on her lips. "The dream is going to be important to you, Ivy." She went over to the desk in the corner of the family room and pulled out a pen and note paper.

"Important?" I asked.

"Significant," she said, writing quickly on the note pad.

"Okay." I glanced over at Cypress to gauge her reaction.

Cypress frowned, crossing her arms. "What exactly did you see?"

Autumn knelt down in front of the coffee table, making notes with her big curvy handwriting. "In my dreams, you're always standing in an outdoor area and there's all this loose dirt. You're holding your camera, taking pictures. There's a wall of stacked stones, and something *else*... but I can't ever see it. It's hidden from me."

I nodded. "So me, my camera, and loose dirt."

"Loose dirt, like from the construction site?" Cypress asked.

"Good point," Autumn said to Cypress, then continued. "I also get the impression of other people standing around... but they aren't building anything." Autumn blew her bangs away from her eyes. "My dreams aren't always clear. When they are like this— a jumble of images— it frustrates me." Autumn doodled on the page as she talked. "I'm sorry. I wish I had clearer images and more specific information for you."

Autumn tore the page free and handed me the paper. I saw the words: Ivy, camera, stones, and foundation. "Don't worry, Watson, I can crack the case."

Autumn snorted out a laugh. "Smart-ass."

I glanced back at the paper and my cousin's doodles. Stars, crescent moons and the letters N and P were the drawn on the side of the paper. "What's N P stand for?" I asked her.

My question got drowned out in the uproar of

Morgan running back into the family room. He threw his arms around Autumn where she knelt on the floor. "Oh no!" she said, playfully rolling as if he had tackled her.

"Dinner is ready!" Great Aunt Faye called from the kitchen.

Lexie and Bran entered the room, and Lexie scooped up her son. Before I could follow the family into the dining room, Autumn got to her feet and caught my hand. "Promise me Shorty, that you'll keep me in the loop with all of this."

"I'm five foot six. I'm *not* short," I said.

"You're shorter than me." Autumn gave my hand a squeeze before she let me go. "You're also nosey. So promise me that you'll be smart, and that you'll be careful."

"Always." I tossed her a wink and followed Cypress into the kitchen for dinner.

Dinner was as usual, loud, with several conversations happening across the table at once. I felt so much better at the manor surrounded by family. Cypress sat next to Aunt Faye and was telling her about her classes. Lexie and Autumn were discussing the vegetable garden in the backyard. Bran tried to cajole Morgan into eating his dinner, and Merlin the family cat sat under my chair until I snuck him a green bean. The cat trotted off with a happy chirping sound, green bean in his mouth, to go and "kill" the cooked vegetable in private. Merlin had a thing for green beans. What can I say, the family cat— familiar is a little special.

Morgan decided he didn't like spaghetti, but he loved the meatballs. Unfortunately, he had a meltdown when Bran cut them up into smaller manageable pieces for him.

Lexie cut off her son's toddler tantrum with three firm words. "Morgan John Bishop."

Behold the magickal power of the full name... I thought.

My nephew's bottom lip quivered as he watched his parents trying to decide how he could get what he wanted. "Broken," he said, looking at the cut up meatball in utter dejection.

I couldn't help it. I laughed. I tried to cover it up with a cough when Bran gave me the stink eye. *Goddess help them both, the kid was a handful.* To hide my smile, I wiped at my mouth with a dinner napkin.

I felt bad for Morgan, he was a happy little boy most of the time, and I could tell he was upset. So to make him cheer up, I focused on his sippy cup and like I'd done earlier with Cypress' water bottle— I made the bright blue cup slide across the tray of his high chair.

All around me dinner returned to whatever passed for normal at the manor. The rest of the family hadn't noticed, and continued with their meal. Morgan blinked at the cup. He tentatively reached for a handle. With my left hand in my lap under the table, I gestured, and his cup zipped over to the opposite side of the tray.

The toddler jumped and frowned at his wayward

cup. I twirled pasta around my fork with my right hand, kept my expression bland, and waited for him to reach for the cup again. He didn't disappoint me.

This time I made the cup slide away to the opposite side of the tray, turn and go right back into his outstretched hand. Morgan smiled and grabbed the handle, drinking out of the cup like he hadn't ever seen juice in his life. After a few greedy swallows of the contents he banged the cup back down and reached for a green bean on his plate. I concentrated hard, and all the green beans on his plate stood on end and wiggled.

I'd have probably gotten away with it if the little guy wouldn't have gurgled in delight.

"Ivy Esther Bishop." Aunt Faye's voice was tough as nails.

Uh-oh. I cringed, and the beans dropped back onto my nephew's toddler plate. *Whether you were two or twenty, the invocation of the full name worked.* With an effort, I tried to act as innocently as possible. "Yes, Aunt Faye?" I blinked as if confused, for effect.

"Behave yourself." Aunt Faye frowned at me.

I flinched when Autumn reached under the table to poke me in the ribs. "Troublemaker," she chuckled.

I tossed my hair. "I have *no* idea what you are talking about."

Lexie rolled her eyes, and Bran seemed to be on the verge of a lecture. I saw him take a breath to begin, so I tapped into my powers and made my dinner roll shoot across the table— right at my brother's head. He snatched it neatly out of the air with one hand. "For Goddess sake, Ivy," he sighed.

I smiled in appreciation. "You've still got pretty good reflexes."

Bran set the dinner roll down deliberately. "I've had plenty of opportunity to practice over the years."

Morgan began to kick his feet and giggle at the flying food. "My Ivy." He beamed at me from across the table.

I blew my nephew a kiss. "You never know..." I said to Bran. "Morgan might be telekinetic like me; you need to keep those reflexes sharp, just in case."

Lexie dropped her head in her hands and groaned.

***

Later that night I lay on the top bunk in my dorm room, listening to Cypress mutter in her sleep. I heard her roll over and murmur something about squirrels, and I smiled. I tried to relax and to will myself to sleep, but my mind was too full of the day. If it wouldn't have sounded so freaking dramatic— I'd have said a storm was coming. Still, Autumn had promised me that she'd privately bring Bran up to speed on that negative energy, and where it seemed to be coming from. And I supposed that should make me feel better... but it didn't.

My intuition was insisting that something was very *wrong*. And sometimes that inner knowing is one nagging, annoying bitch.

With a sigh, I selected the white noise app on my phone, put in my earbuds and told myself to get some sleep. My alarm seemed to go off a moment later. I tapped the snooze icon on the phone screen and threw the covers over my head to block out the sunlight. *God I hated mornings.* I had only dozed back off when the covers were rudely yanked away from me.

"Rise and shine, sleepyhead!" Cypress sang, pulling the earbuds out of my ears. "Ivy, come on. You're going to be late."

"Go away or die," I told her.

"Your vampire tendencies don't scare me," Cypress announced and yanked open the curtains. Bright daylight splashed across my face.

I covered my face with my arms and listened as Cypress bounced around the room all good cheer. Knowing she'd hound me until I was up, I yawned and sat up slowly, my feet dangling off the top bunk. I focused on her, my witchy BFF, roommate and torturer all in one. Cypress was already dressed for the day and her coffee machine was rumbling to life.

"How in the hell can you wake up so cheerful?" I complained, scrubbing both hands through my hair. "I'm telling you Cy, it's unnatural." I climbed over the end of the bunk and staggered across the floor.

"It's aliiiiive!" Cypress exclaimed as she stood before the mirror, adding blush to her cheeks.

I pulled my top lip back from my teeth and hissed at her.

Cypress cringed away. "Ack! Morning breath!"

"Bitch," I said half heartedly and elbowed her out of the way of our shared sink. Cypress laughed at me while I splashed some water on my face and brushed my teeth. Once I was finished I went straight to our little mini fridge, grabbed a can of soda, and popped the top.

"How can you drink a soda right after brushing your teeth?" Cypress asked me for maybe the millionth time.

I started chugging. "Cypress," I said, coming up for air. "I believe that those sorry and sad folks— such as yourself— who wake up early, all bright eyed and chipper should be rounded up and publically flogged in the town square. Say around noon?"

Cypress laughed at my snarky comment. I went back to my soda, guzzling until half the can was gone. I focused on Cypress and, to annoy her, I belched. It was deep and loud enough to make any Frat boy proud.

Burping finished, I patted my belly. "I may live," I said.

"Ivy!" Cypress laughed at the burp, sipping delicately at her coffee.

"You do caffeine your way, I'll do it mine." I yawned again, grabbing my shower bag off the hook behind the door. I scooted my feet into my flip flops, and headed for the showers across the hall. I only felt slightly more enthusiastic when I returned.

"It's the shambling dead!" Cypress joked.

I made a face. "Yeah, that never gets old," I told her,

unwrapping the towel from my hair.

Cypress hitched her book bag over her shoulder. "Your phone was ringing while you were out."

"Okay," I yawned and started to brush out my hair.

"See you later!" Cypress waved and bounced out of our room, slamming the door behind her.

I flinched at the loud noise, but the caffeine had started to do its job and I was slowly becoming more alert. After drying my hair, I went over to my bed and patted around for my phone. I had a voice mail from the editor of the campus newspaper. They wanted me to go over and photograph the construction of the museum expansion.

That's convenient. Now I had an excuse to go snoop around and see if I could figure out what was going on over there at the site. I made a mental note to go over to the site magickally loaded for bear. *I could wear the tourmaline to combat negativity...* I tossed a pop tart in the microwave to warm it up and considered what other things I could do to protect myself from the negativity that seemed to be coming from the area.

I hauled my makeup bag to the mirror over the sink and began to put on my face. Once I had my foundation finished and set with powder, I opened a huge palette of eye shadows and started to add highlight to my brow bones. I went for pale pink under my brows, with a rosy purple for the lid, plum for the crease, and finally a smoky gray to add depth. The colors would bring out the green of my eyes and in this one thing, I took my time. *I loved makeup*... okay it would be more accurate to say that I *obsessed* over eye shadows. I added some deep charcoal eye liner, smudged it into a thick cat eye and brushed on black mascara.

Satisfied with my face, I added my favorite silver pentagram pendant and slid a chunky bracelet of protective black tourmaline over my left wrist. I checked the contents of my camera bag. Making sure I had a fresh memory card, I went ahead an attached my long-range lens to the camera body. I tucked my wallet and keys in the camera bag— today it would have to double for my purse. I stopped at my desk and considered my collection of tumbled crystals and stones that were mounded in a blue ceramic dish.

I chose tiger's eye, hematite, and a snowflake obsidian. All protective stones. I held them up into the beam of morning sunlight that poured in my dorm window. The stones seemed to glisten as they rested in the palm of my hand.

"By the power of protective stones times three; warded, shielded and safe I surely will be," I chanted. I focused on the stones and felt them growing warm. Satisfied that they were now empowered, I dropped them in my camera bag.

I slid my cell phone into an outside pocket of the bag and decided to come back for my books for my afternoon classes. I layered a long, flowing, charcoal striped tank over a black camisole, tugged on black shorts, and laced up my chucks. I hitched my camera bag over my shoulder, remembering my student ID badge at the last second, and clipped it to my top.

I checked my reflection and grinned at what I saw. "Intrepid girl photojournalist— reporting for duty." I added a gray rolled brim hat, angled it low over my eyes and decided I appeared appropriately gothic, and photojournalistic all at the same time.

I hated to admit it, but the late morning stroll across campus perked me up. The leaves of the dogwood trees were starting to show a hint of the red they'd become, and I stopped along the way to take some photos of the foliage. The trip probably took me twice as long as it should have, but I figured the photos would be great for my next photography class project.

I framed my next shot, stepped back and took several pictures. I changed the aperture on the camera and tried a few more. Keeping the camera up to my face, I moved to my left circling the old twisted dogwood tree, searching for the perfect angle, the perfect composition.

I bumped solidly into someone. "Watch out," I said, but never lowered the camera.

"That's very rude," a male voice pointed out.

"Um hmm," I agreed, and stuck my elbow out to help the person move out of my way.

"Hey!" the guy laughed and nudged me back.

I lowered the camera and peered up at him. *Wow, he's gorgeous,* was my first thought. The second was: *I'd love to photograph him.* He was a good six inches taller than me, with light brown, jaw length hair that ruffled in the breeze. His brows were dark, almost horizontal, and made his steel-blue eyes stand out.

I gave him the once over, wondering whether or not I could get his picture without pissing him off. He wore faded jeans and old motorcycle boots. His khaki colored shirt stretched over a great chest, and those steely eyes narrowed at me in derision. *Yum.* My mouth watered. "Stand over by the tree. Lean against the trunk," I said spontaneously.

"What?" he sputtered.

I grinned and tugged him towards the dogwood tree. "Relax, this won't hurt a bit," I said.

"Are you nuts?" he said, scowling at me.

"Nope. My family had me tested," I said. When he only stared at me, I took that for permission. I lifted my camera, took a few steps back, and framed him in.

"You can't just take my picture," he began.

I snapped several as he continued to scowl, or maybe the correct term was glower at me. *Whoa baby. That's one hot glower.* I thought. "Do you want to be responsible for hampering creative genus?" I said completely serious, as I continued to take his picture.

"Listen Goth-Girl," he sneered, and now I felt a little tickle of attraction. He held up his hand to block me, and I lowered my camera. "I don't know who you think you are—"

"I'm Ivy. Hi." I smiled, reached out to that hand and shook it. "I'm a photographer on my way to cover an assignment for the University paper."

He pulled his hand free. "Okay, Ivy—"

"And what's your name?" I asked, cutting him off again.

"Certifiable..." he muttered, struggling against laughter. He shook his head, hitched his leather satchel over a shoulder, and walked away from me as quickly as he could.

"See you around, Certifiable!" I called cheerfully after him.

I watched him break into a jog and chuckled. "Oh man, he was hot!" I said, checking my camera to see how the unplanned pictures had turned out. *Too bad he doesn't have a sense of humor to go with the looks.* I studied a particularly good picture of his glower. *Then again,* I thought. *Glowers really worked on some guys.*

I shrugged and made my way over to the construction area. Even though I had the protective stones with me, I could feel the negativity emanating from the site the closer I got. My mood plummeted, and I reminded myself to raise up my shields. *Go forward in awareness,* as my mom used to say.

I had to wonder how many *other* psychically sensitive people on campus were picking up on this "energetic nastiness." Being exposed to this type of negativity for any length of time wouldn't be good for anyone, be they Witch or mundane. I had a hunch that though the energy had begun on the astral— the plane where magick lived— as it leaked over into the physical plane it would start to cause damage in the "mundane" world.

I blew out a breath, rolled my shoulders against my discomfort, and walked around the history building where the current museum was located. I cut through their little gardens, my stomach churning from the closer proximity to that negative energy. I was relieved to find myself all alone in the pretty gardens. I saw several opportunities for photos, so I stopped and knelt down for a few pictures of a cluster of late summer asters.

I was lowering my camera when an implosion on the astral plane detonated. While silent on the physical plane— the implosion was devastating on a magickal level. The force of the energy was like a punch to the gut. It hit me so hard that I lost my balance and landed hard on my rear end.

Instinctively I reached for my pentagram and held it up on its chain like a shield. My silver pentacle shone bright against the magickal energy that screamed violently around me. A bright golden shield emanated from the pendant into a cocoon of protective energy. It took effort, but I held my ground, pushing back against the negativity that howled past. I was shocked to see the delicate asters next to me being stripped of their purple petals.

As quickly as it had begun, it was over. "Whoa," I gasped. "I've never seen a protective shield manifest visually before." I stayed where I was, scanning the area around me. Allowing the camera to rest against my chest, I climbed carefully to my feet, still holding up the pentacle out in front of me— just in case. *The energy wasn't here anymore.* I realized, with no small amount of relief.

"That was intense!" I muttered to myself. "Any magick user in the vicinity would have felt that." I was reaching for my phone to check in with Bran and Autumn when I heard the first shout.

It was male, and it sounded terrified. I tucked the phone back in my bag, grabbed onto my camera and ran towards the voice.

I skidded to a halt at the edge of the construction site. A large section of the cyclone fence had been taken down, and they had started to dig out for the new building's foundation. Several men were rushing towards one fellow who was down in a scooped out section. They were trying to haul him up out of the area, and others were talking excitedly. As I watched, the equipment was shut off and all of the workers congregated around the man.

I saw no one else in the area, so I walked right through the opening in the fence. The men were about fifty yards in front of me, and I worked my way over quickly. Even though I was nervous from the psychic implosion, I was very curious as to what all of the men's excitement was about. My intuition told me that no one was hurt, but *something* had really frightened them. The closer I got, the more comments I could overhear.

"Holy shit! Do you see that?" the man they had pulled out of the hole said.

"Tim went down to get a better look..." Another man in a bright orange hard hat seemed to be patting the hauled up man on the back.

"Somebody should call the cops..." I heard from someone else.

I quietly skirted around the outside of the group. *You don't even see me...* I pushed a little reluctance out in front of me. It combined nicely with the fascination over whatever it was they'd found, and no one even noticed me. I walked farther around the group, raised my camera lens, and focused on whatever was down in the hole. At first, all I saw was some stacked stones sticking out of the dirt, and a round stone, partially uncovered. I adjusted my lens and took several pictures of a man who knelt down and gingerly brushed soil away from the round stone with his gloved hand.

I jolted when I realized what I was seeing. *The round stone had eye sockets.* It wasn't a stone at all. It was in fact, a human skull. Unexpectedly, a psychic scream seemed to reverberate through my head. Not sure if I was hearing my own horror, or sensing someone else's, I blocked it out, knelt down to changed my camera angle, and kept taking pictures as fast as I could.

"Hey you! What do you think you are doing?" A male voice shouted.

I took a few more shots before I lowered my camera. "I'm taking pictures for the campus newspaper," I said to an angry man wearing a buffalo plaid shirt.

He marched straight towards me. "This is a construction zone, you can't be in here." Buffalo plaid shirt guy scowled and grabbed ahold of my arm.

"Okay, okay, I'm going!" I said, as he yanked me to my feet. "Take it easy."

"Out. Now," he said, hauling me roughly towards the opening in the fence.

"Hey! Hands off!" I pushed a little magick at him and plaid shirt guy stumbled hard enough to release my arm. He went down to one knee. I stepped around him and headed out.

"I'm going to call the police, young lady!" he threatened.

"You should." I turned back to him. "Be sure and ask for my sister-in-law, Officer Lexie Proctor-Bishop." When he sputtered at me, I raised the camera and focused on him. "Say cheese," I said, and snapped his picture.

CHAPTER THREE

I found the highest point on the outside of the fence to take more pictures. The police had arrived, and as if I'd conjured her up, the responding officer *was* Lexie. There were suits out at the site now. I wondered if they were detectives, or maybe folks from the University. I saw a couple of men show up and step into white zippered protective jumpsuits. They tugged shoe coverings on before climbing down into the hole with various tools, supplies, and cameras.

Now things were getting good. I focused my long range lens and took several photos of them brushing away at the skull to reveal more of it. There were other bones too, it seemed. I swallowed past the lump in my throat and told myself a real photojournalist would not be squeamish about bones. The second man in white blocked my shot, and I lowered the camera. My mind raced as I wondered how old the remains were.

My intuition announced my cousin's presence a moment before her hand dropped on my shoulder.

"Ivy." Autumn gave my shoulder a little squeeze. "Felt that implosion earlier, did you?"

"Yeah, that was a hell of a disturbance on the astral plane," Autumn agreed. "What's going on down there? Was there an accident on the construction site?" she asked.

"No." I started to flip through the images on my digital camera. I found the best one of the construction worker uncovering the skull. "They found something." I turned the camera so she could see the digital screen.

Autumn took the camera, and frowned down at the image. "That's a human skull," she whispered.

"I know," I said.

"See how discolored it is? I bet that's *old*. How'd you get such a clear, close up photo?" Autumn asked, with a thoughtful expression.

I shrugged. "I was *inside* the site when I took that picture."

Autumn shut her eyes. "I don't suppose it occurred to you that walking in a construction area might be dangerous?"

"They weren't even paying attention to me, not at first. I got some damn good shots before they hauled me out."

Autumn handed me back the camera. "Your innate nosiness might get you into serious trouble one of these days," she pointed out, crossing her arms over her bright blue blouse.

"I was assigned to photograph the construction for

the University paper. So I'm thinking— right place right time." I lowered my voice before I continued. "I was walking up when I felt the big *boom* on the astral, and right after that, all of the men started shouting."

Autumn frowned at the group of construction workers, campus security, suits, and the police that had gathered. "How long have the police been on site?"

"Half hour maybe?" I raised the camera and focused again. *Weird psychic implosion aside, the campus newspaper would be thrilled with the pictures.* I thought. *Maybe I could land a photo credit for the local William's Ford Gazette.*

While I tried for another good shot, I saw the big guy in the plaid shirt talking to Lexie. He was gesturing broadly and scowling. He pointed right at me. As I watched through the lens, she followed the man's gesture and focused on me. Lexie crooked a finger. She wasn't smiling.

"Uh-oh. I think Lexie wants to have a word with you," Autumn said.

I lowered my camera and glanced over at Autumn. "Aw, hell."

With my cousin quietly lecturing the whole way, I made my way to the opening in the fence at the construction site. "I have a hunch that those remains are not modern," Autumn said. "However, the site is going to be treated as a crime scene, so behave yourself."

I nodded, letting her know I understood, and we stopped at the entrance. A security guard from the

University was waiting for me, and he escorted me over to Lexie.

Now that I was back on the site, I detected a very different mood. No one seemed upset or concerned. There was, however, a buzz in the atmosphere. Almost a palatable excitement. Whatever they police had discovered had changed the mood from horror to curiosity.

Buffalo plaid shirt guy swung around and pointed at me. "That's her," he sounded pretty proud of himself.

"Thank you," Lexie said calmly. "I'll take it from here."

The guy sneered as he walked away. I fluttered my eyelashes, and blew him a kiss when he passed. Surprised, he promptly tripped over his own boots.

I chuckled and walked up to Lexie. "Hi ya, Lexie." I angled my neck trying to see around the people blocking the excavated area.

"Explain to me what you were doing taking pictures inside a restricted area." Lexie scowled.

"Is it restricted?" I glanced around knowing full well there were no signs announcing it as such. I tipped my hat back, scratched my forehead, going for an innocent, vibe. "Golly, I guess I missed seeing the signs."

The man in the orange hard hat stepped up and shook Lexie's hand. "Hello, I'm the construction site manager. The signs hadn't arrived as of yet, but I guarantee you they will be posted on the construction site. Today. I will see to it myself personally."

"Your construction site is now our crime scene," Lexie informed him. And I had the pleasure of seeing the man's jaw drop. "Until the Medical Examiner releases the scene, we are treating it as an active crime scene." Lexie scanned the man's ID badge that hung from his shirt. "I'll tell you what— Steve. We are going to want to interview everyone who was involved with discovering the remains. If you could round those people up for me. I'd appreciate it."

The man's chest puffed up importantly. "I'm happy to help in anyway that I can." He walked away.

I grinned at Lexie. "Well that was smooth—"

"I'm going to need those photos, Ivy." Lexie cut me off.

I clutched my camera protectively. "I was assigned by the campus paper to photograph the construction... you can't take my photos!" *No way was I going to let that happen!*

Another man walked up wearing a suit and tie. He was dressed more formally, but my first impression was that he too was a cop. "Hello, I'm Detective Johnson," he introduced himself. "I understand you were photographing the site at the time the remains were found?"

Lexie flared her eyes at me in a silent warning to be polite. "Yes sir," I said respectfully. "I was covering the construction for a story for the University paper."

"I'm sure that you are protective of your photos, however according to Dr. Meyers from the University, those photos might be important to any future research or archeological excavation," he said.

"Archeological excavation?" I asked. I glanced back at Autumn who was hovering outside the fence. *Damn, the girl called it! Score another one for the Seer.*

"Ivy," Lexie's voice was low. "The skull and the other bones... they are discolored, meaning they're more than likely *very* old. The ME could tell that almost immediately."

"Oh, did they accidentally dig up an old grave?" I asked, trying not to sound too excited.

An older gentleman walked up. I recognized him as Dr. Hal Meyer. Autumn worked with him at the museum. He was a nice older gentleman and was practically quivering in excitement. "Hello Miss Bishop. Lovely to see you again." He eyeballed my camera as he spoke to me. "Would you be willing to share your photos with the future archeological team? As I was telling the detective, the photos would be invaluable to their research."

Well when he put it that way... "I'd be happy to share. *If* I'm given the photo credits, and I retain all the rights to the photographs."

"I'll take care of that personally." Doctor Meyer nodded at us, and turned away to answer his cell phone.

"Is that a digital camera?" Detective Johnson asked conversationally.

"It is," I said.

"Would you please show me the photos that you

took?" he asked pleasantly.

I glanced up at Lexie, she nodded, and I scrolled through the pictures for the detective. He noted the number of a few of the pictures, 57 through 64 and asked me to email them to him. He handed me a card and excused himself.

I considered the guys in the zippered suits down in the hole. I raised my camera, focused and snapped several shots of them as they worked.

"Okay, that's enough." Lexie caught my arm and steered me towards the opening in the fence.

"Aw, come on Lexie!" I said. "Let me get a few more—"

"Do you want your camera confiscated?" Lexie cut off my protest.

I clutched the camera protectively to my chest. "You wouldn't!"

Lexie escorted me to where Autumn stood outside of the fence. "Wait here," she ordered, and walked over to Detective Johnson for a brief word with him.

I slanted Autumn a look. "You were right on the money. They said the remains were old."

"I spoke to Dr. Meyer," Autumn said. "He's very excited, even though this will probably put a halt to the construction for a few months."

"Will you get to help the archeology team?" I asked.

Autumn shook her head. "No, I'm not a physical anthropologist."

"Okay..." I frowned at her words. "Why aren't you a

physical anthropologist? What's that mean?"

"Simple answer?" Autumn said. "I don't deal with bones."

"Oh," I said, working hard not to make a face over the word, *bones*.

Lexie marched back over to us. "Okay Ivy, let's go," she said.

"Go?" I blanched for a moment imagining being hauled off to the police department.

"I'm escorting you to the nearest computer where you will email both me and Detective Johnson the photos he's requested. If you do that, you are allowed to keep your camera and its contents."

I sighed. "The simplest way would be to use my laptop. It's back at my dorm."

"Excellent." Lexie took me by the arm. "You've earned yourself a police escort back to Crowly Hall."

Autumn burst out laughing. "Call me later," she said.

"Hey!" I winced when Lexie clamped down firmly on my arm. "Sheesh, Lexie," I said as she quickly walked me to a squad car and opened the back door for me.

Unexpectedly, Lexie put her hand on top of my head and pushed. "Watch your head," she said, shoving me into the backseat.

I barely got my feet inside before she smartly shut the door.

I checked the door, it was locked. I couldn't get out. I rapped on the glass with my knuckles. "Are you freaking kidding me?" I yelled.

Lexie stood there in the bright sunshine and grinned. "This way you will stay out of trouble for a minute." Lexie seemed way too cheerful as she waved goodbye to Autumn and climbed in the driver's seat.

I crossed my arms over my chest and glared at the back of my sister-in-law's head. "Police brutality," I muttered.

"I heard that," Lexie said, and with a cheerful whistle she started the car.

When Lexie pulled up outside of Crowly Hall everyone stopped and stared. "Oh my Goddess!" I rolled my eyes, mortified, as Lexie double parked the car in front of no less than a dozen of the residents. And sure enough... a bunch of the girls had whipped their cell phones out and were snapping pictures.

Of me.

Sitting in the back of a squad car.

Lexie got out, went to the passenger door, and opened it for me. "You're lucky I didn't have the lights or sirens on," Lexie said with a straight face.

I resisted the urge to hold up my hands to show the other girls that I wasn't wearing cuffs. I straightened my shoulders and strolled right up the front steps with Lexie. "Hey, Leann." I nodded to the girl whose room was right across the hall from mine.

Leann stopped texting and stared at me slack-jawed as I strolled past her.

Oh man, I would never live this down...

Fifteen minutes later, Lexie had gone. I'd simply inserted the camera's card into the media slot on my laptop and emailed the requested pictures to Detective Johnson and to Lexie at their police department email accounts.

Now that I was alone again, I downloaded all the pictures to my computer and started to scroll through them one by one. I skimmed past the cute, scowling guy I'd met earlier and went right to the important shots. Taking a critical study, I decided number 58 was the best of the lot. The angle of the photo, the line of the construction workers back as he brushed the soil away from the skull with his gloved hand. *Yeah, that one was the best.*

Now that the adrenaline rush was fading I realized something else. *I hadn't noticed any other negative energy from the construction site while I was there.* Meaning whatever had been there— was now released.

I thought back to the energetic implosion I'd experienced and reached for the silver pendant I wore. The pentagram had been a gift from my mother when I'd turned thirteen. I held it up to the light and considered. *I'd never seen the pendant manifest magick physically before.* For a moment I felt very close to my mother, and grateful for the protection of the pendant she'd given me.

When that energy had howled past, I'd been untouched. My hat hadn't been blown off; my hair hadn't even rippled, while the flowers next to me had been stripped. Grateful to have been wearing the protective talisman, I pressed a kiss to it.

"Thanks Mom," I said, letting the silver pentagram drop back around my neck.

***

My favorite photo, number 58, made the front page of the local newspaper, the campus newspaper, and a few websites. I was interviewed by the local paper too, but honestly I was more thrilled with my photo credit. Cypress clipped the pages out of the papers and pinned them to my bulletin board for me, teasing me about being a glory hound.

Crowly Hall gossip had run hot and fast for two weeks about my involvement in the discovery of the remains. I'd heard everything ranging from that I was a suspect in a murder investigation, to I'd fallen into the site and had to be rescued— and my personal favorite, that I had made the bones appear by means of some dark magick spell.

Cypress had laughed uproariously over that last one. I'd told her that in this day and age there was simply no excuse for the general public not to be aware of, or educated, about the Craft and Paganism. I'd never been on the down-low about my religious beliefs or my family's legacy of magick— and over the years this meant I kept my closest friendships limited to other practitioners. Sure, I saw the occasional open-minded mundane guy, for fun and casual dating only. Like my mother had before me, I mostly kept to my own kind.

I was proud of my heritage. It was a part of who I was. While I was basically considered to be a prodigy due to my telekinetic powers, in other areas of the Craft, such as spell casting, I was pretty mediocre. My magick would grow, change, and evolve over time, but Witchcraft would always be a part of my life.

I thought back to how shocked Autumn had been the first time I used a locator spell on her... which was simple magick, and something most Witches could pull off without a fuss. Even working alone. Holly and I had been a part of a magickal duo for eighteen years. Without my twin, I floundered with my spell casting. Truthfully, I had the best outcomes to my spells when I worked *with* another Witch, like when Autumn and I had broken that binding spell that had been on her a few years ago.

I yanked myself out of my inner musings and glanced down at my shirt. It was black (of course), and today's slogan was, *I'm only here to recruit girls for my coven.* Sure, it made some people walk a wide berth around me. Not to mention Aunt Faye would have launched into a lecture about me needing to be more subtle if she would see me wearing such a thing. But it made *me* smile. Understated it was not, but at least it showed that I had a sense of humor.

I knew that eventually the hoopla over the discovery at the construction site would fade. I only had to wait it out. In the meantime I would wear whatever I damn well pleased, and keep to my normal schedule. I'd done my very best *not* to cackle at the fellow residents of the dorm for the past few weeks. That had to count for something, right?

The good news was the psychic implosion I'd felt when they'd discovered the remains hadn't occurred again, and the negativity I'd originally discerned on campus had dissipated. For the time being, Bran was quietly doing research on the history of that particular area of the campus. Autumn had a line on any future information on the archeological dig from Dr. Meyer, Cypress and I were getting into the routine of a new semester, and for some reason... I felt like I was waiting for the other shoe to drop.

My unease had been building over the past few hours, and out of habit, I reached for the silver pentagram pendant. After the implosion I hadn't taken the necklace off. While the pendant seemed to be behaving itself and acting like an average piece of jewelry lately, I still didn't want to switch it out with another necklace. Not even for another magickal symbol.

The pentacle had protected me. It made me feel like my mother was watching over me, and I was leaving it on. Rolling my shoulders against the tension that had gathered there, I tugged my earphones off and stretched in my desk chair. It was almost midnight, I'd been studying for hours.

"I'm calling it," I said to Cypress.

Cypress rubbed her eyes. "Yeah, that's enough for me." She closed her notebook and began to put away her books.

I let myself quietly out of our room, heading for the restroom across the hall, when one of our new residents walked smack into me. "Hey," I laughed, reaching out. "Watch where you are going there, girlfriend."

She never acknowledged me in any way. The girl walked slowly on in her pink pajama shorts and sleep shirt, and right past her room.

"Was that Jessica?" Cypress asked, coming to the door.

"Jessica?" I called softly.

Cypress stepped around me. "I think she's sleepwalking."

My curiosity got the better of me. I walked quickly to her side and gently reached out to touch her shoulder. "Jessica?"

She stared at me with her eyes open and I felt a chill roll down my back. My mind raced as I considered what I should do. *You weren't supposed to startle a sleepwalker awake, were you?*

Cypress stepped forward. "Your room is back this way." Cypress gave her a gentle nudge back in the right direction.

"Okay," Jessica said, wandering back the way she had come.

We waited until she went to her room and Jessica

stopped still in front of her door. I saw the door was open a crack so I pushed it the rest of the way open, and Jessica went in.

I closed the door and we started back. We'd almost made it to our room when the lights in the hallway all began to buzz and flicker.

"What the hell?" I glanced over at Cypress.

Cypress shivered. "Damn, it's cold all of the sudden."

I heard a door open and once again Jessica appeared in the hallway. She walked right past us and towards the top landing of the stairs.

"Hey!" I called, rushing after her. I grabbed her arm and yanked her away from the edge of the steps, hard. Hard enough to have woken her.

Jessica turned blank eyes towards me. "Do you hear her?"

"Hear who?" I asked as Cypress joined us.

"She's calling." Jessica stood staring off into space. She tried to tug her arm away from me as if she would go down the stairs.

"Who's calling you?" Cypress asked.

"The Headmistress." Jessica continued to try and pull away from me.

I tried to ease Jessica away from the top landing. "There's no one talking. You're dreaming." I glanced at Cypress. "Cy, give me a hand."

Cypress reached out and helped me to pull the struggling girl farther away from the stairs. Above us the security light sizzled and popped.

"I have to go to her!" Jessica strained against us.

"Jessica, stop fighting me." I shook the girl's arm. "Wake up!"

Jessica jolted awake blinking furiously. She frowned at Cypress and me, and as we watched, her eyes refocused. "What's going on?" she said.

"You were sleepwalking," Cypress told her.

"I was?"

Cypress put her arm around the girl. "Come on. It's okay. Let me walk you back to your room."

I trailed behind them, and saw that the hall lights were now burning true. Cypress escorted Jessica back to her room, and I ducked into the restroom across the hall. By the time I came back Cypress stood waiting, hip shot and arms crossed.

I shut our door behind me and leaned against it. "What the hell happened out there?"

Cypress tilted her head. "I don't know, but the lights stopped snapping and blinking when Jessica woke up."

"Yeah, I noticed that too. The cold, the blinking lights. Cypress, that's like ghost type stuff."

Cypress blew out a breath. "We're talking true paranormal activity."

"She said the *Headmistress* called her." I scratched my chin. "Would that be our resident ghost?"

"The stories of Victoria Crowly's ghost have always been benevolent," Cypress said.

"As far as we know." I pointed out.

"We've lived here in the Hall for two years, and never experienced anything like this before." Cypress shrugged.

"Which makes me wonder, why now?"

Cypress yawned. "I could do some research. Ask some of the ladies from the historical society, and see what they know about the history of the campus haunting."

I rubbed my hands over my face. "I have to work at the shop tomorrow. Between customers I can do an internet search, see if I can find anything."

"Sounds good," Cypress said.

Satisfied with our plans we both went to bed. I climbed up the end of the bunk bed, flopped face down, and was asleep in moments.

CHAPTER FOUR

During the school year I worked at *Enchantments* on Friday and Saturday afternoons and every other Sunday. Great Aunt Faye now ran the business side of things-mostly from home. The old girl seemed to enjoy the ordering and purchasing of items for the shop, and she liked to come in on Tuesdays and an occasional Saturday to help run the counter. However, she was *conveniently* never around when it was time to unload the shipments, stock the shelves, or to do any cleaning.

Those tasks fell to our full time employee, Teri, and also to Autumn and me. Cypress had also picked up a part-time job at our shop. So the family's business ran smoothly. Teri had decided to re-arrange the layout of the store earlier this summer, and the four of us had given the place a complete overhaul.

The day after the creepy sleepwalking/flickering lights incident at the dorm, I was manning the front counter. I'd been using the store's computer and had been unsuccessfully searching the internet for stories about the haunting at Crowly Hall. Most of it was simply urban legend stuff, with no proof to back it up. I printed out a few short articles, but there wasn't much of anything to most of the stories. They were mostly anecdotes. I did read several interesting online articles about paranormal investigation. I printed out the best one and added it to my stack.

I wondered at the lack of customers in the shop. Even though there was plenty of foot traffic on Main Street, it was surprisingly quiet. I decided to freshen up the front window display, but after that, I was still bored. So I fussed with the bowls of tumbled stones on a table, and caught my reflection in the mirror on the brick wall.

"I'm digging the cloudy blue." I decided, tugging at my shirt. *The Moon* tarot card was emblazoned on the front, and the loose top draped off one shoulder. It framed the tattoo on the back of my shoulder, nicely. The tattoo had three small stars around a slim waxing crescent moon, and was a stylized version of the Bishop family magickal crest. To go with the lunar theme I'd added dangly silver crescent moons earrings, and my silver pentagram pendant glistened against the gray-blue of the shirt. Comfy, distressed denim shorts peeked out from beneath the slouchy top.

I'd made a conscious effort to start adding more color to my wardrobe lately. I was still getting used to it. Truth was I wore a lot of black, and rarely any other color. I supposed some folks might find the lunar ensemble a bit too much— but for me— it was downright subtle.

The ticking of the old clock sounded unusually loud this afternoon. I wandered over to the front windows again, and frowned. *Why was it so quiet in the shop? We were usually busy on Fridays.* I moved away from the window and considered working a little prosperity magick to drum up some business.

I was starting to organize the supplies for my spell on the front counter, when Cypress dropped by.

"Hey, do you have a minute?" Cypress asked, walking in. She wore a short, swingy bright coral dress. A heavy, silver fleur-de-lis pendant hung around her neck.

"Yeah, it's been really slow this afternoon." I moved out from around the counter. "You look nice. Big date tonight?" I wiggled my eyebrows at her.

Cypress smiled. "Jake's going to pick me up at Marie's in a little while."

"Marie wants to meet him?" I grinned imagining how Cypress' aunt would probably scare the crap out of Cypress' newest boyfriend. "Good luck with that."

Cypress rolled her eyes and hitched her large, colorful bag higher on her shoulder. "Yeah anyway, I have some information about our ghost in residence."

"I did a little digging myself today. Read up on paranormal investigating. Found lots of urban legend stuff, but maybe a few leads." I gestured to the comfy reading chairs that had been set up in front of the used book section of the store. I plopped down in one of the chairs. "Lay it on me," I told her.

Cypress sat in the other chair, smoothing her skirt over her knees. "I went to the museum on campus and had a chat with Dr. Meyer."

"He's such a cool old guy," I smiled. "I bet he talked your ear off about the history of the campus ghost.

"He did have a lot of information. Did you know he wrote a book about it?" Cypress reached into her purse and pulled out a slim paperback.

She handed me the book and I quickly thumbed through it. "This is great. I'll use it with the stuff I pulled from the net."

"What did you find online about the ghost?" Cypress asked.

"Well there's a bunch of urban legend type of things. But there are a few older articles about the ghost of Victoria Crowly. In the 1970s some girl was actually interviewed in the Gazette about her experience."

"What happened to her?" Cypress asked.

"She said the ghost saved her. Claimed that she kept her from falling down the stairs— as in from the third floor. Apparently there were about a half dozens girls who saw the whole thing."

"Oh wait, he did mention that story to me." Cypress took the paperback again, and thumbed through it. "Yeah, it's right here." Cypress pulled a receipt out of her purse to mark the page for me.

"So the ghost has been helpful to the residents in the

past?"

"I flat out asked Dr. Meyer if there were any claims of the ghost luring people out of their rooms." Cypress shrugged. "He seemed pretty surprised by my question."

"I found accounts, or stories of people spotting her in the Hall," I said. "A few students have also claimed to see a woman in white around Victoria Crowly's grave on campus over the years."

"Dr. Meyer told me she was a *benign* presence," Cypress said, handing me back the book.

"Yeah, most of the stories handed down in the Hall are of her being protective of the residents. Almost motherly." I tucked my hair behind my ear as I thought it over. "But I figured that was to keep the residents of the Hall from being afraid."

"Besides an occasional sound in the attic... we've never had any problems with her," Cypress said.

"Well, where the hell was the old girl last night?" I joked. "We could've used a hand with Jessica."

"Before I go, there's something else I wanted to tell you," Cypress said. "There was a serious accident at the excavation site today."

"Oh. Sorry to hear that. Who was it?" I asked, thinking of all the people I had seen working over there for the past few weeks.

"I don't know. It happened after Dr. Meyer gave me the book. He rushed out and went straight over. People were pretty upset. When I left the museum, the ambulance was already there." Cypress stared down at her hands and fidgeted.

Her body language made me frown. "What's got you worried Cy?"

"Things feel weird to me," Cypress said, meeting my eyes. "Ever since they found those remains. Energetically, things feel off."

"What happened last night creeped us both out." I set the paperback down. "I'll admit, I keep seeing Jessica's blank face." I blew out a breath and said what I was thinking. "I have a feeling that if I wouldn't have stopped her last night... Jessica would've pitched herself down the stairs."

Cypress shuddered. "I've been thinking the same thing."

I reached out and clasped Cypress' hand. "We need to keep an eye on things at the Hall."

"Agreed." Cypress nodded. "Do you want to cast a protection spell on our dorm? We could do it together."

I pursed my lips as I considered. "Well, that's actually manipulation. Unless we get every single resident's permission to cast a spell for them."

Cypress snorted out a laugh. "Not too likely."

"Why don't we batten down the hatches in our room for starters," I said. "Then we'll keep watch and see how it goes?"

Cypress left a short time later, promising to pick up some supplies for the protection work from her Aunt Marie. The shop stayed quiet after she left, so I skimmed through Dr. Meyer's book. I took a few notes on the more interesting stories of sightings of Victoria Crowly's ghost.

By the time five o'clock rolled around, my stomach was growling. I tucked the book and all my notes in my purse and started to run the closing reports. With Bran, Lexie and the baby out of town for the weekend, and Aunt Faye up in Hannibal visiting friends, my original plan to nab some takeout, stop by the manor to feed and water Merlin, and spend the evening watching a DVD in solitary splendor didn't seem very appealing to me anymore. I felt the need to be around people, and noise.

I finished the closing paperwork and let myself out the front door of the shop about a half hour later. The September sun slanted down brightly as I locked the front door. I stuck my big, black floppy hat on my head and checked my reflection in the display window. I dropped the keys in my bag and fished my compact out. I reapplied some lipstick in a matte crimson shade, and powdered my nose while I was at it.

I stowed the cosmetics, pulled the brim of the hat down a bit lower, and, satisfied with my appearance, strolled off, comfortable in my black converse sneakers. There were plenty of restaurants and bars doing a brisk business tonight, I noted. I could always pop in somewhere and grab a meal. Then afterwards, I'd drop by the manor. Following my intuition, I turned left and started to wander.

I'd maybe gone a block when I spotted *The Old*

World Pub. A popular establishment with both locals and tourists. I saw that tonight the outdoor seating was full. But as I glanced through the windows, I found two empty spots at the far end of the bar. I tugged open the heavy wooden doors and waved at the hostess, she nodded and left me to seat myself.

The bartender, Miriam, flashed a smile as she placed a menu in front of me. "Hey, it's my favorite goth girl."

I tipped my sunglasses down. "I'll have a Dr. Pepper, dah—ling," I over pronounced the word for dramatic effect.

"Good day at the shop?" she asked.

"Quiet today." I tucked my sunglasses in the neck of my shirt.

"The new window display at the shop is great. I saw you working on it when I came in to work today." Miriam set a soft drink in front of me while I perused the menu. I ordered a club sandwich and sweet potato fries, and sat at the bar chatting with Miriam, and swinging my foot in time to the Irish music that was playing.

Casually, I scanned the other patrons. At a tall four-top table a trio of Frat boys sat together drinking beer and talking loudly. They were borderline obnoxious, and all probably newly twenty-one years old.

While I couldn't scan their minds like my cousin Autumn, or even read their emotions like my twin sister could— I didn't have to. The energy they were pushing out was rude, and just this side of drunk. They called loudly for their waitress and I saw Miriam give a little head shake to their server. *The boys had been cut off.* I shifted slightly in my chair, acted as if I hadn't noticed them. I lifted my pentagram from my shirt and slid it back and forth on my chain while I thought over my conversation with Cypress.

A moment later the last remaining barstool was claimed, and I glanced over to see a man wearing a navy blue bandana tied around his head. He had straight brown hair that peeked out of the bottom of the headscarf. He wore khaki shorts, work boots and a purple University t-shirt. I guessed he'd probably been working outside all day. I appreciated the view and smiled at him when he turned on the bar stool to look me fully in the face.

His dark, horizontal brows lowered, and steel blue eyes blinked at me in recognition. "You," he grumbled.

"The name, is Ivy," I said, my heart doing a little dance. He was every bit as attractive as he'd been that day I'd photographed him, scowling at me under the dogwood tree. I dropped my pendant, and raised an eyebrow at him.

He narrowed his eyes. "No camera today, Ivy?"

"Nope." I spread my hands. "See? I'm unarmed."

He laughed at that. "I feel safer already." As I watched, he seemed to catch himself. He ordered an iced tea from Miriam, glanced back at me, and the smile slid away.

Why was he fighting the laugh? I wondered. *It did*

wonderful things to his face. I smiled at him anyway. "I never did catch *your* name."

He picked up a menu, studied it with determination. "No, you didn't," he said straight faced.

Stymied, I drummed my fingernails against the bar top. "Are you always so unfriendly?" I asked him.

At my question he lifted his head and met my eyes. His gaze dropped pointedly down to the large silver pentagram my mother had given me, and back up to my face. "I'm not your type," he sneered.

The disapproval I felt from him hit me harder than I would have expected. I'd encountered versions of the same criticism, and or narrow-mindedness since I was thirteen. *Maybe it was the gothic fashion, my snarky attitude, or possibly the pentagram that was putting him off...* it really didn't matter. I sighed, gesturing to Miriam. "Can you make my order to go?"

He silently rolled his eyes at me and reached for his tea.

I tugged my wallet from my purse to settle the bill. By the time I'd pulled out the cash, my food was in a bagged to-go box— like magick. I handed Miriam the money. "Keep the change," I said.

I stood and gathered my food. "Have an enchanted evening," I said, as he set the drink back down. I pulled my hat down more securely on my head, and with a flourishing gesture, made his glass of iced tea slide farther down the bar. He blinked, and did a double take.

"Humph." I sailed out of the pub with my nose in the

air.

What an asshole! I stomped back down Main Street. *I should have made his drink tip over in his lap while I was at it...* I smiled, cheered at the thought. *Too bad about the condescending attitude— not to mention the permanent stick up his ass, because he was one of the best looking guys I'd met in a long time.*

The crowds thinned out as I walked closer to *Enchantments*. The sun was behind the buildings now, and I ducked down the brick alley to take a shortcut to our little parking lot behind the store. As I stormed back to my car, I worked out a dozen clever, pithy comebacks that I could have said to Mr. Congeniality.

I was digging in the bottom of my purse and my fingers had only folded over the car keys, when I heard steps behind me. I saw the three Frat guys from the pub were standing at the top of the alley. And they were staring at me. *Shit.*

"Where you going, witchy-girl?" The tallest of them flashed me a smile.

"Don't be shy!" the second one called out as they started to lurch down the alley towards me.

"I'm not shy— just not interested," I said, walking to the hood of my old red Fiesta. I had the keys out, but before I could get to the drivers door to unlock it, the third guy came around from the back of the car. They had boxed me in.

"Don't be so unfriendly," the third guy said.

Hearing my own words repeated back to me made

me sick to my stomach, *and* it really pissed me off. I dropped my purse, keys, and the food so my hands would be free, "You boys have made a major mistake." I planted my feet and flung both hands out to my sides. Magick filled up my hands with an almost visible energy.

"Waz that?" One of the guys pointed at my hands.

He must be a sensitive, or the alcohol had lowered his shields. Regardless, I swung my eyes back and forth, wondering who to zap first. I struggled to maintain control, even as I closed my fists around the energy and prepared to strike out defensively.

Suddenly guy number three was pulled back and away from me. He went tumbling backwards and fell hard on the blacktop. I blinked and discovered that my rescuer was none other than the scowling, bandana wearing, Mr. Congeniality.

"Walk away," he growled at the two remaining Frat boys.

"Actually, I'd run if I were you." I turned towards them, blocking my rescuer's view. I threw my hands forward and open simultaneously, and my magick shot out hitting *exactly* where I'd intended. The two remaining guys bent over as one, each clutching their balls. They stumbled away from me as fast as they could.

I watched the three of them stagger off, and as soon as they lurched up the alley I let myself exhale. I steadied myself against the hood of the car with one hand and squinted up at my rescuer. "Thanks for the assist," I managed as black and white spots swam in front of my eyes. My ears buzzed and I felt slightly sick.

"Hey!" he gave my shoulder a little shake. "Are you okay?"

"Yeah." I'd never raised and thrown defensive energy on my own that quickly before, and I fought to stay upright. *Holy crap,* I thought. *Maybe I should stick with telekinesis, because this throwing energy solo shit really knocks you on your ass.* I blinked and shook my head to clear it. "What are you doing here?"

"I saw them follow you out of the Pub," he said.

I suddenly realized he was still holding my arm, and I tried to pull my arm away. "Why the hell would you even care?"

He let go of my arm immediately, and held up his hands. "Easy, easy. I was simply concerned for you."

I squinted up at him and said nothing.

"Look, if you walk around dressed like a girl from the coven in that TV horror show..." his words trailed off.

I clapped a hand to the crown of my floppy black hat and pushed it back down in place. "What the hell is that supposed to mean?" I said, firing up again.

"It means that you're bound to attract the wrong kind of attention." He scooped up my purse and the bag of food from the ground and held them out.

"Think you've got me pegged, don't you?" I saw my

keys lying in the gravel a few feet away. "You know *nothing* about me." I said, holding my hand out. I used my telekinesis and the keys shot straight up hitting my hand with a loud snap— right in front of him.

He jumped back from me. "God damn it! You *are* a real practitioner!"

I blinked at his choice of words. "Yes, I am. And you sir, are a real asshole." I unlocked my car, snatched the bags away from him, and tossed my things inside.

"Wait." He grabbed the car door before I could get in. "Hang on. What's your family line?" His voice was low and urgent.

"Dude, what is with you?" My head was still spinning, both in reaction from the self defense magick, and from his conflicting reactions.

"You caught me off guard. Your last name, what is it?" he asked.

I scoffed at that. Telling another magickal practitioner your full name was not something that was casually done, because names held power. "Do I look like a novice?" I raised my eyebrows.

"Yes actually, you do." He scowled down at me, even more disapproving than before. "You use your powers out in the open, and you dress like a wanna-be."

Returning the favor I looked him over, deliberately. "Such a harsh critique from an obvious fashion icon... I'm devastated."

He almost smiled. "Who are you?"

"Give me your name first," I countered.

"Nathan Pogue," he said.

Nathan Pogue. N P... I realized with a jolt. *Autumn had doodled those initials on the side of that note paper she'd given me the other day.* I stared up into those steel-blue eyes, and despite myself felt a little tingle all the way down to my feet. I covered it with attitude. "And your family line?" I asked, narrowing my eyes at him.

"My lineage comes from my father's Irish ancestry and from my mother's family— Osborne."

I recognized the old Colonial name. *So... Mr. Congeniality's mama was descended from the earliest of American Witches.* Straightening up, I met his eyes. "My family line includes Jacobs and Bishop," I said quietly and with pride. "My name is Ivy Bishop."

I watched his eyes widen as my announcement sank in. He drew in a long breath. "You're a *Bishop*? By the old gods..."

His reaction made me feel offended all over again. "Jerk," I said, shaking my head at his shocked expression.

"Is Bran Bishop your brother?" Nathan asked

"Yes," I said, scowling up at him. Technically, Bran was my cousin, but my mother had adopted him when he was little, which *also* made him my brother. But this was hardly the time, the place, or even the person to whom I'd consider explaining the complicated twist of my family tree.

"I need to speak to your brother, right away," he

announced.

I'd had enough intrigue for one day. Instead of answering him, I ducked under his arm, climbed in my car, yanked the door out of his grasp and started up the Fiesta.

His polite knocking on my window was the last thing I expected. "Ivy," he said.

"What?" I shouted over the engine.

He motioned for me to roll down my window. "Listen, we need to talk. I really have been trying to contact your family."

I didn't roll down my window to answer him. Instead I cranked up the car stereo to blasting as he tried to continue speaking.

"Did you hear me?" he frowned at me.

I smiled when the song changed over to Meghan Trainor's, "NO." "Sorry, can't hear you." I mouthed the words to him, pointing to my ear.

He stood there gesturing wildly and obviously trying to shout over my music. I put my car in gear and backed up. I flipped him the bird, and whipped out of the parking lot. I headed straight to the manor, singing along with the song, never looking back.

CHAPTER FIVE

Merlin was waiting for me in his sentry position on the kitchen island when I arrived, and greeted me with a loud meow. I hung my hat on a hook in the potting room, carried my dinner into the kitchen, and went straight to the cat for some kitty comfort. I knew better than to scoop him up for a cuddle, Merlin wasn't big on being held. So I leaned over and laid my forehead against his nose. "Hey Merlin." He rubbed his face against mine, and gave a playful nibble to my hair.

I dropped a kiss between his kitty ears. "I had an interesting afternoon," I said, opening up my dinner. I was happy to find that with a little re-stacking, the club sandwich was fine. I snagged a soda out of the fridge and climbed on a barstool to eat my dinner, discussing the events of the day with Merlin.

Going back over what had happened, I had to wonder... *Why had Nathan said that he'd been trying to contact my family? If Nathan wouldn't have identified his lineage, I'd have never guessed that he was a practitioner. Or was he? Maybe he was simply a magickal snob.* While I mulled that over, a white tipped paw reached out and batted at a sweet potato fry. "You won't like it," I warned the cat.

Merlin ignored me and tried again. "*Aus!*" I told Merlin, and he let go of the waffle fry immediately. I pulled a small piece of turkey from the last of my sandwich and offered it to him instead. "*Fass*," I told the cat, and he snatched the meat so fast that I started to giggle.

A few years ago, after the big smack-down with the Drakes and the BMG, I had secretly taught Merlin attack dog commands... in German. The fact that Merlin was a cat and that I didn't speak German as a rule seemed to make no difference to our fifteen pound familiar. He'd taken right to them. Suddenly the cat whipped his head around in the direction of the front door and hissed.

"What's wrong?" I asked, watching him. I reached out with my intuition and felt someone approaching the manor... Someone uninvited. "*Zur wache!*" I gave the command to be on guard, and Merlin took off with a growl towards the front of the manor.

I got up to follow him and barely made the family room before there was a loud, demanding knock on the front door.

I reached out with my magick to try and sense who was out there. I picked up on impatience and frustration, but no ill intent. I walked through to the foyer and eased up to the front door, quietly leaning forward to check the spy hole.

Nathan Pogue stood on my front porch, and wonder of wonders he was still frowning. I didn't even bother to wonder how he'd known where I lived. *If* he was a practitioner, that sort of locator spell would be child's play for him... and if he wasn't— well all he had to do was ask around. I stepped back, debating whether or not to ignore him. Merlin let out a warning meow and leaned against my leg. I glanced down at him. "Should we see what he wants, Merlin?"

Merlin's bright golden eyes met mine. He blinked and titled his head as if to say, *Your call.*

"*Sitz,*" I told Merlin, and he sat obediently next me. To be safe, I took a deep breath and pushed some of my own energy into the household wards to reinforce them. I tapped my fingertips three times on the doorframe. "By all the power of three time three," I whispered. "Impenetrable my home will be." As I finished the verse I saw a little bolt of yellow light run along the doorframe.

I thought about how I wanted to play this, and I started to grin. I knew exactly how to handle the gorgeous— pompous— I corrected myself. The *pompous* ass. I grounded my energy planted my feet, and opened the door.

He tugged the bandana from his head and twisted it in his hands. "Hi," he said.

"Well my goodness," I drawled in my best southern

accent. I fluttered up at him, fanning my face with a hand. "It's a gentleman caller."

He closed his eyes at my snark and took a breath.

I could tell he was counting. I'd experienced similar frustrated reactions from my own family over the years. After a ten-count, he opened his eyes and focused on me. "Ivy, I need to speak to your brother. Is he home?"

"He's out of town." I kept hold of the door, staying on my side of the threshold.

"What about the relative that works at the museum? Her name is Autumn, isn't it?"

"And you'd know that how?" I demanded, my protective instincts kicking in. *If he thought he could skulk around and spy on my relatives... he was in for a world of hurt.*

He held up his hands and took a half step back. "I met her the other day."

I scowled at him. "Tell you what, why don't you leave me your number and—"

"This *is* important," he cut me off.

"I'm sure *you* think it is," I said.

He drew himself up. "I was simply hoping to have a private, polite conversation with an elder member of your family line."

"Really?" I shot back. "You should probably go home and practice being polite first. From what I've seen that's going to be a real challenge for you."

He did a double take.

I stood silently and waited.

"I'm sorry," Nathan said, rolling his eyes. "I apologize for my behavior—"

"Too late!" I sang.

"—this afternoon," he said over me. "It's been a hell of a day."

"Let's add 'learning to sound sincere' to your to-do list," I suggested, crossing my arms over my chest. "Why are you really here, Pogue?"

"I told you..." He leaned in aggressively, closer to the door. "I was hoping to speak to a member of your family." He stared down at me. Our eyes locked and I felt a trickle of his power.

I broke eye contact, and yanked my head back. *The sonofabitch had just tried to spell me!* I had a flash of insight and realized that he was used to getting his way. *By his looks, or his magick.* I glanced down at the cat. "*Achtung*," I said quietly. Beside me, Merlin let out a feline grumble and rose up to attention.

Nathan's jaw dropped open at that. "Did you really give your cat a command— that it obeyed?"

"What's the matter? Too subtle for you?" I said over the increasing volume of Merlin's growl. I stood up straighter and held my ground. *No way was he getting past the wards.*

"This isn't getting us anywhere..." Nathan scrubbed a hand over his head, and his hair fell artfully around his face. His whole demeanor changed as he braced his forearm against the doorframe. "Why don't you invite me in?" he practically purred, leaning in closer with a slow smile.

The open space in the door frame— and between us — lit up with a bright yellow flash. He fell back from the door, and I had the supreme satisfaction of watching his jaw drop for the second time that day.

"Manners, Pogue. You really do need to learn some," I said, stepping further back into the foyer. "I'll be sure to let my family know that a pompous asshole from an east coast line of Witches dropped by." I flicked a finger towards the door. Untouched it began to swing, and slammed shut— right in his face.

I focused on the lock and it flipped loudly. I waited until I heard him leave and I rushed to the family room window. I stood off to the side, watching him stalk down the front sidewalk. He let himself out of the narrow opening in our tall, iron gate at the end of the driveway, barely clearing it— when it banged closed behind him.

From the window I could see him flinch in surprise, spinning around to scowl at the gate. Merlin jumped up on the windowsill and made a chirping noise that sounded like a chuckle. We watched as he got into his little black sports car and drove away.

I stepped away from the window. "What an asshole! Why did he have to be so good looking?"

As an answer, Merlin took a swipe at my hand.

"Ouch!" I yanked my hand away and inspected it. "Well at least you didn't break the skin." I glared at the cat. "I never said I *liked* him."

Merlin radiated feline superiority and began to groom his paws.

I couldn't help it. I started to laugh. The whole scenario struck me as outrageously funny. "What a day." I went back to the kitchen, still chuckling. I cleaned up my dinner and fed the cat. I snagged an ice cream sandwich out of the freezer and headed upstairs.

Going directly to the hidden panel in my brother's closet, I tugged down on a brass hook and the door swung open. I selected a volume on the original Witch families from the colonies and went back to my room to study up.

I settled into the curved window seat and stretched out my legs. I flipped open the book and, while I ate the ice cream, started reading about the earliest of the Witch families in America. I had a hunch I'd be seeing the gorgeous, rude, and ill-tempered Nathan Pogue sooner than later.

I wanted to be ready when I did.

***

In hindsight I probably should have found a more discreet way to fill my cousin in on the events of the previous afternoon. I tracked her down at her part-time job at the local history museum and slipped in to her office as quietly as possible. I hadn't seen Autumn get really angry in a long, long time. But even though she didn't raise her voice, I had to admit... it was a hell of a show.

"Someone tried to do *what*?" she growled, while above her the fluorescent lights began to flicker.

"I said, some ass-hat named Pogue, from an East Coast line of Witches, tried to charm his way past the wards at the manor yesterday."

Autumn jumped to her feet. Her desk chair went rolling back and bounced off the wall. "Why didn't you tell me right away?" she demanded.

I shifted my black, loosely crocheted poncho over the emerald green cami I wore and sighed. "I tried to catch you this morning before you left for work."

"Damn it Ivy!" You should have called me last night!" she said, and the little task light on her desk blew out with a pop.

"Hey, hey, ratchet that down." I reached out. "Relax before you blow out all your computer equipment." I patted her arm. "I told you I was fine. He couldn't get past the wards."

Autumn seemed to catch herself. She closed her eyes and inhaled deeply. "Start at the beginning. How did you meet him?" she asked.

"I first bumped into him on campus a few weeks ago..." I filled Autumn in about how I'd met him right before the skull had been discovered. Then how he'd helped me with the drunk Frat boys. "He didn't approve of me. Said I dressed like a wanna-be and had *no* subtlety."

"Guy sounds like a prince," Autumn said, scowling.

"He never explained exactly why he wanted to speak to Bran?"

"No. Only that he'd been trying to reach him." Above us the lights stopped their frantic flashing. "He also said that he knew you. That he'd met you." I tipped my head to one side. "I'm guessing he met you at the museum?"

"Describe him to me."

"He's about six feet tall, with straight brown hair—" I gestured to my jawline. "Down to here. He'd be nice looking if he wasn't such a pompous asshole."

"Pogue..." Autumn went back to her desk, and began riffling through a file.

"Nathan Pogue," I said.

She held up a paper. "I *did* meet him. He's one of the grad students working on the archeological excavation."

"Well that explained the work clothes he was wearing," I said.

Autumn shifted over to her computer and began typing. "Got him," she said a few moments later. "He started with the Master's program this year. Nathan Pogue, from Danvers, Massachusetts."

I walked around her desk to join her. "Danvers?" I wondered, reading his file for myself. "Isn't that close to Salem, Massachusetts?"

Autumn glanced back over her shoulder at me. "Very. It's less than five miles from modern day Salem."

"Why do you say, *modern day Salem*?" I asked.

Autumn leaned back in her desk chair. "The Witch Hunt hysteria actually began in what was called 'Salem Village'... which is known today as— Danvers, Massachusetts."

"So things are suddenly hinky, we have a new player in town, *and* he comes from the place where the Witchcraft trials originated from?" I shuddered. "That can't be good."

"No, it's not. I want to check something..." Autumn trailed off and began an online search.

Curious, I leaned into my cousin, peering over her shoulder again. I saw that Autumn had pulled up a few documents listing the names of the people imprisoned or executed for Witchcraft during the hysteria. "What are you thinking?" I asked.

Autumn tapped a few keys and began to print the files. "I'm starting to think— like your mother always said— *there's no such thing as coincidence.*" Autumn nudged me back and grabbed the papers from the printer. She pulled a hot pink sharpie out of her desk drawer and began to mark the pages she'd printed.

Fascinated, I went and sat in one of the little office chairs, pulled my denim clad legs under myself, and watched her go to work. "When you lived in New Hampshire, did you ever make the pilgrimage to Witch City?" I asked, leaning my elbows on her desk. *I'd always wanted to see Salem, the place famous for the Witchcraft trials.*

"Sure. Salem is a pretty harbor town filled with fabulous history," Autumn said, never even glancing up at me. She opened a yellow sharpie next, and began to highlight different sections of the page.

"Did you see the old graveyard, and the Witch Trials Memorial?"

"Yes, my father took me when I turned thirteen." Autumn blinked up at me. "He took me out of school for the day. The two of us played hooky... and we never told my mother." She smiled as she reminisced. "We went to all of the museums, and toured the House of the Seven Gables. Saw Gallows Hill... And wow, I suddenly realized that he must have been trying to sneak in *something* about the legacy of magick, in a roundabout historical way." She sat back and blew out a breath.

I watched her shake her head at the memory. "I wasn't trying to make you sad," I said.

"You didn't." She smiled at me. "No worries, Shorty."

I knew she was a little touchy on the point of her father. He'd hidden her legacy, and even bound her magick. I stuck my tongue in my cheek, hoping to make her laugh. "So, did you ever sneak out with your friends and go back to Salem around Halloween?"

Autumn grimaced. "Only once. It's frantic, loud and crowded during the month of October. The best time to go is in the summer, when you can see everything without all the crush of crazy tourists dressed in cheap costumes." She switched out the highlighters for a ball point pen and began to make notes on the back of a page.

"Show me what you're doing," I said.

Autumn spread the papers out on the desk. "Ivy, check this out," she said, pointing at the names she had highlighted. "Notice anything familiar about the names?"

I resisted rolling my eyes. Bran had taught me the history of the earliest Witch families years ago, *and* I'd spent last night boning up on them. "Sure, I see some very familiar names: Bishop, Proctor, Jacobs..."

"What was the line Pogue told you his mother came from?" Autumn asked.

"Osborne," came a male voice from the doorway.

I turned in my chair, and saw Nathan Pogue standing inside the door of Autumn's office, and for once he wasn't scowling. His eyebrows were raised and his mouth was set in a smug line. He was obviously staring down his nose— at me.

"Well, well." I lifted an eyebrow at him. "Speak of the devil."

Nathan stood there confident in pressed khakis and a blue button down shirt. "My mother's line comes from the Osborne's. They originated in Danvers— what was once known as Salem Village," he said proudly.

"Am I supposed to applaud?" I asked him.

Nathan glared at me in reply.

Autumn took the printed pages and tucked them into

a folder. She casually stuck the folder in her desk and rose to her feet. "Come in Mr. Pogue. Please shut the door," she said politely.

I resisted the urge to laugh and gave serious consideration to diving under the desk for cover. Autumn didn't "do" a soft and controlled tone of voice. *This was going to be good.*

Nathan stood for a moment, then shifted, closing the door behind him. "I was trying to contact Bran Bishop, the eldest male of your family line. However I've been informed he is out of town..."

"Correct." All business and polished in her black jacket, ruby colored top and slim dark pants, Autumn walked around her desk.

Nathan shrugged and tried a smile. "Well if that's the case, I suppose that I'll have to settle for speaking to you." He held out a hand.

I hissed out a breath at the condescending attitude.

Autumn cocked her head to one side, her lips curling up slightly. She ignored the offered hand. Instead she walked right up and got into his face.

Nathan stepped back automatically and came up short against the door.

"You're new in town," Autumn said pleasantly. "Let me give you some advice. The Witches of William's Ford stand together, and on equal ground. We do not defer leadership based on gender."

Nathan stiffened. "I wasn't trying to cause offense."

"Yet you did so, *brilliantly!*" I pointed out.

Nathan swung his gaze to me, then back to Autumn. "I apologize."

Autumn stepped back, easing out of his personal space. "Sit down Pogue." She gestured to one of the chairs in front of her desk. "And state your business."

Nathan waited until Autumn sat back behind her desk. After she sat down, he took the empty chair next to me. "I have some concerns about the incidents that have been occurring at the site."

"Such as?" Autumn didn't give an inch.

Nathan shot me a sideways look. "There's a lingering energy that remains at the site. Stronger than any other dig I've assisted with."

Autumn and I exchanged glances.

Nathan leaned back in his chair. "Yesterday there was a serious accident on site. One of the archeology team members broke their leg."

"I know," Autumn said.

Nathan crossed his arms over his chest. "I was there when the accident happened. The archeologist's injury occurred when they were in the process of removing items for analysis from the site."

"So did they fall or something?" I asked him. "What has you so spooked?"

"She didn't fall, the ground caved in under her," Nathan said.

I suddenly *knew*. "The person who was hurt, she was taking the human remains off site. Wasn't she?"

"Yes." Nathan seemed surprised when he met my

eyes. "The ground opened up right beneath her... It was the strangest thing I've ever seen. And the injury... it was ugly."

"Ugly?" I asked.

"It was a compound fracture, Ivy," Autumn said. "Dr. Meyer told me about the accident this morning."

I swung my gaze from my cousin to Nathan. "While they helped the injured woman... what happened to the human remains?"

"I volunteered to transport them back to the lab at the museum," Nathan said. "They are currently being stored here."

I shuddered. "You couldn't pay me to go anywhere near those remains."

"They're only bones, Ivy," Autumn said soothingly. "You shouldn't—"

"There's more." Nathan's voice was so serious that it made my hackles rise. "I wanted to discuss this with your brother..." Nathan seemed to catch himself. "But I will be happy to discuss this with two current members of the Bishop line."

Autumn nodded. "Go ahead."

"Yesterday was not the first incident at the excavation. There's been a series of accidents at the dig," Nathan said. "With the latest being the worst. *And* it happened when they were removing the last of the human remains from the site." He blew out a breath. "Now, some of the people working on the excavation are getting nervous. A few students have even quit the dig."

"Hmmm..." Autumn seemed to consider.

"Full disclosure?" I tilted my head at my cousin.

"Go ahead," Autumn said. "Tell him."

"There was some sort of psychic implosion when the skull was first found on campus." I explained to Nathan about my experiences that day. When I'd first become aware of the negativity, the energetic blast I'd felt, and the photos I'd taken of the discovery.

"*You* are the photographer Dr. Meyers has been talking about?" Nathan asked with raised eyebrows.

"Yes, I am," I said. "You seem surprised." I managed to resist making a face at him.

"The photos? I've seen them. They're very good," Nathan said.

"Be still my heart." I pressed a hand to my chest. "Was that a compliment?"

"Grow up," Nathan shot back.

"Knock it off, you two," Autumn said. "Getting back to our timeline of events...The discovery of the skull halted the construction of the museum expansion," Autumn said. "It closed the site, while the M.E. did his analysis."

"Right." Nathan nodded. "Then the archeological department took over and began to excavate the area."

I scratched my head as I thought it over. "You've all been working on the area for a couple of weeks now, right?"

"Yes," Nathan said. "There's something else. And it

concerns me. Word on campus is that the site is cursed."

"Oh, perfect," I said, rolling my eyes.

Autumn leaned her elbows on her desk. "There are plenty of locals who know the magickal history, and current activities of the families in town," she said. "A chain of incidents and a serious injury at the archeological site? That's bad, and people on campus *are* starting to talk about it. People have even been whispering about it all morning here at the museum."

Nathan nodded. "Not to mention that if enough people start to believe in a curse at the site, they could literally *think* it into being."

"First of the Hermetic Laws: *thought creates*," I said, thinking about the foundational principles of magick.

Nathan whipped his head around. "Did you really quote the Hermetic Principles?" His eyes were wide, and he was clearly surprised. "You?"

I sneered at his air of disbelief. "Want me to rattle off all seven of them?"

He blinked at me, and then slowly turned to my cousin. "So are we in agreement that this bears further magickal investigation?"

"Yes," Autumn said quietly. "I'll need to talk to the rest of the family. Maybe even call in the High Council."

Nathan nodded. "I'll leave you my cell number if I can be of any help. Please don't hesitate to call me."

I watched Nathan write his number down on a piece

of paper and pass it to my cousin. *Don't hesitate to call me?* He sounded so formal and stuffy. His vocabulary reminded me of talking to Great Aunt Faye.

Nathan stood up to leave. "Thank you for your time." He nodded at Autumn, ignoring me completely.

I stood as well. "I'll catch you later." I nodded to Autumn. "I'll walk out with you Pogue." I made an *after you* gesture.

I followed him out in the hall, and we walked silently to the lobby of the building. "You know, you could have told me all of that last night when you dropped by the manor," I said as he opened the outside door for me. "You didn't have to be so dramatic."

Nathan scoffed as I sailed past him. "*I* didn't have to be so dramatic?" He pointed at me. "So says the girl wearing a... what is that? A *cape* or something?"

"It's a poncho, if you must know." I smoothed the fringe down over my hips. "You seem awfully concerned with my wardrobe... Maybe you should be majoring in fashion design Pogue, instead of archeology."

"I'm having a hard time taking you seriously when you look like you are wearing wings."

"It's called a bat-wing style poncho." I smiled at him while he continued to mutter.

Nathan rubbed at his forehead. "What do you think your cousin will do?"

"What she said: talk to Bran and maybe contact the High Council. As for me..." I trailed off and tapped my fingers together. "I think it's time to do a little paranormal investigating. There's a full moon tonight. That's good energy. I wonder what I can dig up?"

Nathan had started to walk away. He stopped and spun back around. "No." He frowned.

"Relax," I said. "I'm not gonna gather the campus coven and whip out the Ouija Board."

"Keep your voice down!" He swung his eyes around, worried we'd be overheard.

No one was paying attention to us, we were alone on the sidewalk. It took everything I had not to laugh. "You know, for a guy that comes from Salem Village, and who trots out his magickal lineage, I would've never suspected that you'd be so far in the broom closet."

"I am *not* a closeted Witch," he said through his teeth. "I do however prefer to be discreet with my magick and my religious beliefs while I am here working on my Masters degree."

"Okay," I smiled at him. "Whatever makes you more comfortable."

Nathan opened his mouth as if to reply and instead frowned down at me. "You don't seriously have a coven on campus?" He seemed slightly horrified at the thought.

I blinked and couldn't resist yanking his chain. "But of course," I lied.

Nathan closed his eyes and seemed to be searching for composure. "I knew I should have waited for your brother." He pointed at me with a scowl. "Don't be stupid. Do not play with things you have no hopes of understanding or controlling."

"You're such a snob, Pogue," I said, lightly.

"By the old gods. I give up." He tossed up his hands and stalked off.

I watched him walk away and reached for my cell phone. Campus coven? No. But I did have my witchy roommate. Between Cypress and me we should be able to get to the bottom of things.

I dialed Cy's number and waited until she picked up. "Hey Cypress?" I said. "How do you feel about a witchy stake out of the campus cemetery and the new excavation site tonight?"

CHAPTER SIX

The full harvest moon rose slowly in the eastern sky. It illuminated the university grounds with an eerie golden light. After hiking around the old theater, Cypress and I walked quietly across the grass to a more secluded section of campus. We cut through the parking lot and made our way uphill to the area where the campus stopped and a nearby church yard began.

Our sneakered feet were quiet as we walked along the winding downhill drive. To our right, on a grassy knoll, were two small cemeteries. Surrounded by old, heavy iron fences, the graves lay silently, illuminated with moonlight.

I hitched my tote bag higher on my shoulder. "It was smart to agree to check out the old campus graveyard first since it's closest to our dorm. We can make our way back over to the archeological excavation afterwards."

Cypress nodded. "After researching Victoria Crowly and her husband Gerald all afternoon, I really wanted to visit her family plot to see if we can pick up anything. Maybe vibes, or a random EVP."

"Too bad Holly's not here," I said, trying to keep the wistfulness out of my voice. "She'd be the best one to sense any emotions or old memories from the area."

"Yeah." Cypress linked her arm through mine. "Have you heard from her at all lately?"

"No," I said and tried to smile despite my disappointment in my sister's behavior.

"Let's go do a little ghostly research, my friend," Cypress declared rather grandly.

"Who ya gonna call?" I said.

Cypress laughed in reply. "Call the friendly neighborhood Witches."

We approached the first plot, but stayed on the paved service road. "You know Cy, we pass by the little cemeteries all the time, but I've never really gave them much thought," I said. "How many folks are buried here?"

"According to my research, there's around twenty people between the two plots," Cypress said, shifting her gaze up to the golden-orange moon. She stepped off the road into the thick grass and headed for the first little cemetery.

"That many?" I said, following along. The night air was becoming cool quickly, I was glad I'd worn the crocheted poncho.

"Yes," Cypress voice became softer as we approached the small fenced in areas. "There's even a few dogs buried here as well."

"The dogs have tombstones?" My interest was piqued.

"Umm hmm." Cypress pulled a small flashlight out of her jacket pocket and a dozen stacked bracelets jingled at her wrist.

The first fenced off burial ground we approached wasn't overly large... maybe twenty five feet square, it boasted a half dozen upright old tombstones. Three or four more markers were lying even to the ground. "Hey, what do you call the ones that are almost flush to the grass?" I asked.

"Lawn markers," Cypress answered.

"Lots of different styles of headstones..." I trailed off.

Cypress shined her flashlight on them. "This is the Harris family plot."

"Harris family?"

"Victoria Crowly's maiden name was Harris," Cypress explained.

"Oh, I hadn't known that." I lifted my camera, made a few modifications and tried to frame the huge harvest moon into the shot of the small cemetery.

Cypress pointed at my camera. "Can that thing take pictures at night without a flash?"

"Sure," I said. "You only have to make adjustments for..." I trailed off as movement in the trees caught my eye. I lowered the camera and checked our surroundings. No one was out walking around this section of the campus. At least no one corporeal.

Cypress walked to the open gate, but did not go inside. As I watched, she crouched down and pulled a plastic baggie out of the pocket of her dark blue jacket. She left a small offering of bread right inside of the gate, where it wouldn't be seen. She said a few soft words I couldn't quite make out and came back to stand next to me. "I left an offering to Baron Cimitierie," she explained.

"Covering your bets?" I said.

"I lived in NOLA until I was fourteen. Where I'm from, we take our graveyards seriously."

"Baron Cimitierie," I tried to pronounce the name as Cypress had. "Is he an aspect of Baron Samedi?"

Cypress grinned. "That's a good way to look at it. Baron Cimitierie is a New World spirit. He guards the bones of the dead at night."

I framed a few more pictures, and we decided to move farther down the hill to the second fenced in plot. This one was a tad smaller and closer to the paved road. I counted eight upright headstones and one big stone box as we walked along. Another waist-high, iron fence surrounded the old family plot. Seven of the stones were very old, and two were more properly called monuments, Cypress explained.

"That one is an obelisk," Cypress said, pointing to the tallest one. "The one next to it? That looks like a pillar with a drape over it? Would be considered a monument. Not a headstone."

"You *do* take your cemeteries seriously," I said, raising the camera to get a few pictures.

"Yes ma'am." Cypress smiled, shinning her flashlight over the largest headstone. It was much larger, thicker, and a more modern style than the rest in the plot. It stood out from the others.

"It's pink," I said, lowering my camera. "Oh god, how tacky..." I tried not to laugh, it didn't seem appropriate. But the granite tombstone actually sparkled in the beam of Cypress' flashlight.

"That's the grave of Victoria Crowly," Cypress said. "They replaced her tombstone sometime back in the 1980s... apparently the original stone had been damaged."

"But it's *pink*!"

Cypress sighed. "Try and focus, girlfriend. We're here to gather information, not critique the aesthetics or to play tourist."

I wrinkled my nose at the modern headstone. "I can't help it Cy. It's silly and out of place next to the older ones." We stopped in front of Victoria's grave, but stayed on the outside of the waist high iron fence to study the engravings.

Cypress shined her flashlight across the stones. "Okay, there's her husband, Gerald Crowly's gravestone," she said, pointing to the old marker to the right of Victoria's.

"I need to come back during the daylight hours to get clear pictures of all the engravings." I followed the beam of the flashlight and discovered that on the opposite end of Victoria's grave was an above ground... crypt, I supposed.

"Hey NOLA girl, would that thing be called a crypt?" I asked Cypress.

"Yes," Cypress said nonchalantly.

The crypt was situated in the top most corner of the fenced in plot. I made my way over, doing my best not to be creeped out by an above ground burial chamber. I beckoned Cy over and she shined her flashlight on the top. I lifted my camera and tried for a picture of the engraving in the beam of Cy's flashlight.

"Melinda Harris Easton." Cypress read the cracked top. "Born 1830. Died 1858. Beloved wife and mother."

"Harris?" I said. "Wife and Mother. I guess she must have been related to Victoria? A sister maybe?"

"Yeah I found some documentation on a younger sister," Cypress said, running her fingers along the edge of the crypt. "There are a few old photos of the boys with Victoria in the books I went through."

"I didn't think Victoria had children of her own."

"She didn't," Cypress said. "The pictures are with her nephews. Melinda's children."

"All boys?" I said, and suddenly I *knew*. "There were three of them, weren't there?"

"Yes, I can show you the pictures. I have the books back at the dorm."

The moon had risen higher in the sky, its color fading from orange to pale yellow. I stood a few feet away from the grave of a young mother, a woman who had only been a few years older than myself, and felt incredibly sad. I knew exactly what those little boys had gone through losing their mother. "Can I have a piece of that bread for an offering?" I held out my hand to Cypress.

"Sure," Cypress said, reaching into her pocket.

I took the small piece of bread and knelt down. The grass was slightly damp, and I felt it seep through the knee of my jeans. Reaching through the spokes of the fence I set the bread in the corner a few feet away from Melinda Easton's crypt. "Baron Cimitierie, I place this offering with respect. Guard over the remains of these people..." I thought about the crack in the top of the crypt. "Protect this place from mischief and harm," I felt compelled to add.

Cypress pulled a mini-recorder out of her bag. "I want to see if we can pick up any EVPs."

She clicked the recorder on and hid it in the tall grass outside of the gate of Victoria Crowly's plot. She pulled her jangling bracelets off and put them in her pocket, her voice was soft but clear. "EVP session. September fourteenth. Time begun, 9:30 pm."

Cy stood and nudged my arm. "There's a spot where we could sit over there. We'd be out of sight to any cars that would drive past. And far enough away from the recorder."

I followed her lead and we strolled past a few haphazard grave markers outside of the fenced-in plots.

Out of respect, we sat well away from the random graves, choosing to sit under a cluster of large trees. We leaned back against the largest tree, where we could watch over the two little cemetery plots. Cypress clicked off her flashlight and we settled in.

There were no cars using the service road along the cemeteries tonight. So it was sort of relaxing to sit and watch the moon rise higher in the sky, the vibe was peaceful and magickal with the Harvest Moon. I tried to pay attention, but after a time my stomach started to grumble. I reached in my tote for the snacks I'd brought along.

"Want a snack?" I whispered, passing her a granola bar.

"Yeah, I'm starving," Cypress said back as quietly as possible.

I pulled a couple of bottles of water out of my bag and handed her one. We ate in companionable silence. I whispered in her ear. "Nice night."

"It is, and the full moon is so pretty," Cypress whispered back. "It's quiet over on this side of the campus." She took a swig of water and capped her bottle.

I leaned close again, keeping my voice low as to not mess up her recording. "I don't think many students come over here, except for Halloween night." I took a drink. "Or the occasional dare to sorority pledges."

"Yeah well," Cypress said softly. "I have never understood the whole fascination with 'let's hang out at the Victoria Crowly's grave expecting to see her ghost thing'."

"Er, Cypress," I whispered. "I hate to break it to you, but that's what we *are* doing."

"We're sitting quietly and respectfully. It's not like we're doing selfies by the tombstone," Cypress grumbled.

"How *bourgeois*," I muttered.

Cypress snorted out a laugh, and promptly clapped a hand over her mouth. Her eyes gleamed in the moonlight.

All of my instincts went on full alert. "Do you hear something?" I hissed.

"Don't joke around, Ivy." Cypress glared.

"I'm not." I pointed to a copse of trees off to our left and further down the hill. I set my water bottle aside and stood. I kept my back to the trunk of the large tree and focused my intuition. *What's out there?* I pushed my abilities out to scan the area. I picked up on laughter, and mischief. I peeked quickly around the trunk and saw a soft blue light shimmer in the trees. I gulped, yanked my head back and sincerely hoped it was students on campus. But the laughter, sense of mischief, and a slight tinkling sound I heard made my blood run cold. *Please don't be Trooping Fae.* That's the last thing I wanted to deal with.

Cy climbed to her feet and by unspoken agreement we leaned around the tree trunk together to visually check the area behind us.

Out of the trees below us came a group of people. Their voices were pitched low, and they were talking excitedly back and forth between themselves. I felt my shoulders slump in relief. The blue light was apparently the screen of someone's cell phone. They climbed up the hill, coming closer and closer to me and Cy, until one of them tripped over a small headstone, making the rest of the group stop and erupt into nervous laughter.

"What the hell was that?" A female voice complained. A light from a cell phone shone on the ground.

"It's a grave marker for a dog," someone answered.

The group sailed right past us. No more than twenty feet away from where Cypress and I stood against the tree trunks, effectively camouflaged by the dark shadows. The girls headed straight for the open gate to the cemetery where Victoria Crowly rested. *What in the hell were they up to?* I wondered. *Were they actually going inside of the fenced area?* Sure enough, I saw the flash of a camera phone and the selfie session with the tombstone began.

I shook my head as the camera phone flashes lit up the area in bright strobe effect. Someone was bound to see that. *There was a reason I hadn't used a flash with any of my photos tonight. Those idiotic girls could ruin any hope Cypress and I had for a paranormal investigation.* I sighed in frustration. Cypress nudged me and pointed. I whipped my head around at the sound of footsteps coming from the right.

"This area is off limits to students after sunset," said a loud, annoyed male voice.

There were a few shrieks, as the group of sorority girls all huddled together inside the plot. As one, they squinted against the beam of a Campus Security Officer's very bright flashlight.

While the security officer berated the group of students, I tugged Cypress down with me to crouch back against the ground. Under the trees it was plenty dark, and we were both wearing dark colors. I hoped neither the guard nor the students would see us. I gave Cypress' hand a squeeze. "Reluctance," I said as quietly as possible.

"You don't see or hear us, we blend right in..." Cypress said under her breath.

"With these words our spell begins," I whispered the final words and our combined energy pushed out, surrounding us. With some surprise I noticed that the sounds of the girl's complaining and the officer telling them to move along, were now muffled. *Nice!* As usual, my spell casting worked better when I had a partner.

A few moments later the group of sorority pledges, voicing their disappointment, were herded away from the plot, and back on to the service drive. The officer began shooing them towards Greek Row.

As the girls moved back down the paved road with the officer trailing them, Cypress slowly leaned close to me. "Damn sorority girls," she breathed in my ear.

I shrugged. "Can't live with 'em, can't turn them

into newts."

"I hope the recorder is okay," Cypress said.

"Let's wait a few minutes make sure the coast is clear and then go fetch it," I suggested.

The only thing we did see moving were a few bats flying around the trees snacking on mosquitoes. We released the reluctance a short time later and stood. I tucked the wrappers away, stowed the water bottles, slipped my tote bag over one shoulder, and followed Cypress to the cemetery gate.

"It's still here," Cypress said with a sigh of relief.

"Was it still recording?"

I heard a click. Cypress grinned over at me. "Yes, it was." She tucked the mini recorder in her own bag.

"Good, we can listen to it later. See if we picked up anything other than the pledges and their selfie session."

Quickly we went back the way we came. Back around the theatre, past Crowly Hall and making the trek clear across campus towards the history building and archeological site. We walked up along the fenced area and gazed down at the excavation. "Wow," I said. "Look at that." A large squared off area had been neatly excavated. The light of the full moon lit up the area very nicely, revealing the remains of a stone foundation of a house. "Foundation... Autumn had said the word *foundation*," I said to Cypress.

Cypress' eyes popped wide. "That's right she did."

My breath hissed out as I took in the remains of an

old house. They've been really working on it, haven't they?"

Cypress curled her fingers through the cyclone fence. "You sound surprised. Haven't you checked on the progress while they've been excavating?"

"No." I shrugged. "I've been avoiding walking too close the area. I even asked the campus paper to assign someone else to cover it."

"Why?"

"I was there the day they found the remains. That was enough for me." I shivered, and it wasn't from the cool evening. I pulled some strawberry licorice from my tote and offered a rope of it to Cypress. We stood eating and watching the site for several minutes. Even though nothing seemed out of place, I rolled my shoulders against the tension. "I think we should head back and check the camera and recorder."

"Agreed. I don't like how the atmosphere feels over here," Cypress said, staring down at the remains of the stone foundation. Deliberately she pulled the copper, silver and gold bracelets from her pocket and put them back on. The bangles had belonged to her grandmother. Cypress liked to wear them for protection. "It feels *off*." She scowled back at the dig. "I wonder why?"

"Maybe that's because you shouldn't be in this area," said a familiar, annoyed voice.

I jolted, but managed to toss a sneer over my shoulder. There stood Nathan Pogue, wearing a distressed brown leather jacket, a white t-shirt and jeans. "Good evening, Mr. Pogue," I said in my most formal tone.

Cypress arched a brow. "So, this is Nathan Pogue?"

"Yup," I said, wondering what she was up to. I'd filled her in on the conversation we'd had in Autumn's office, and about what had happened that day when he'd helped me out in the parking lot with the drunk Frat boys.

Cypress drew herself up, and stuck out her hand to Nathan, her bracelets jingling.

He automatically went to shake her hand, and when their hands met, I watched him jolt. "You're a practitioner as well," he said, focusing on Cypress. "You're a Witch... but there's more," his eyes narrowed as he considered.

"You could say that..." Cypress smiled.

I watched my best friend have an energetic face off with Nathan. Their eyes locked as she clasped his hand, and the bangles on her wrist started to glow slightly. Cypress stored energy in those bracelets, and she could zap adversaries hard with that energy if she felt threatened or was magickally attacked.

Knowing this might take some time, I dug in my bag for the licorice. "Cypress," I murmured after a few moments, "don't fry him."

"We're merely getting acquainted." Cypress tossed her head. "Aren't we, Nathan?" She finally let go of his hand, and stepped back.

Nathan didn't move a muscle. As I'd expected, he

acted like someone had smacked him between the eyes with a two by four. Cypress often had that effect on males. If I didn't love her so much, it would seriously piss me off. I snapped my fingers in front of his face. "Earth to Pogue," I said.

His eyes shot to mine. "I'm sorry, what?"

"Hey." I smacked his arm lightly so he'd snap out of whatever mojo Cypress had used on him. "Have you been following us tonight?" I asked.

Nathan shook his head and eyeballed Cypress, actually taking a step away from her. He turned to consider me. "Following you? Hardly. I was only keeping an eye on the archeological site. Making sure it was protected from vandalism."

"Why? Are you worried someone will break in?" I said.

"With the rumors about the dig being cursed," he said, "I didn't want students to be messing around with, or taking things from the site."

"What would they possibly be interested in stealing?" I asked, genuinely confused. "Stones from the foundation?" I took a bite of the candy.

"Did I overhear you say that you were using a recorder, earlier?" he changed the subject.

"Eavesdropping is rude," I said around the licorice.

"So is talking with your mouth full," he shot back.

"You're as fussy as my great-aunt," I said, slanting my eyes towards Cypress. She was trying not to laugh.

Nathan seemed to pucker up at my comment. "You

have leaves in the fringe of your poncho." Nathan narrowed his eyes at us. "Where else have you two been tonight?"

I glanced down, brushing at the bits of dried leaves. "We were investigating at the campus cemetery."

"What? Why would you do that?" Nathan asked.

"To try and catch some evidence and maybe a few EVPs of course." I rolled my eyes and finished the licorice.

"Gods save me from amateurs," he muttered.

"Oh, and you're what?" I laughed. "A professional?"

"Yes. I've studied parapsychology," Nathan said.

I glanced over at Cypress. "I feel safer already, don't you?"

Nathan pointed at us. "*You're* the ones who got rousted out tonight by campus security."

I gave him my snootiest expression. "No, that would have been the sorority pledges taking selfies by the founder's tombstone in the cemetery."

Cypress flashed a smug grin. "We on the other hand, were sitting under the trees, quietly observing the area," she said. "The group of girls walked right by— never even saw us."

"Neither did the security guard," I added.

Nathan shook his head. "I'm walking you two back to your dorms. You shouldn't be out here," he said.

"Well thank goodness," I said. "A big strong man came along to save us!"

Ignoring the snark, Nathan reached out and snagged

me by the elbow. He started to reach for Cypress and clearly thought better of it. "Cypress," he said politely as she sailed past him.

"We were leaving anyway," I pointed out as he tugged me along.

"I'm sure you were." Nathan followed Cypress through the little gardens beside the history building. "But this way I can be sure you get back to your dorm, safely," he said.

I tried to tug my arm free. "I don't know how I managed before you came along, Pogue."

"I am trying to be polite," Nathan said through his teeth.

Cypress grinned at us from over her shoulder. "Oh honey, it's sweet that you *think* you are trying to be."

"Listen to me," Nathan said, as we all stopped on the sidewalk in front of the parking lot. "I don't believe that the area is safe *energetically*. Especially not for other practitioners, and definitely not under a full moon."

A flash of insight hit me hard. "You think the site was used for dark magick, don't you?"

Nathan's eyes popped wide. "I didn't say that."

"No," I said. "You didn't have to say that. But I *knew* anyway."

"Ivy's an intuitive." Cypress hooked a thumb in my direction. "A very good one."

Nathan shifted his gaze from Cypress to me. He seemed to be weighing his next words. "I think it's very possible some sort of intense magick happened there in the past."

"Something has you scared." I realized.

"Not scared," Nathan said. "Cautious. Very cautious, until I figure out what sort of magick went down in that location."

"And what makes you think *intense* magick went down there?" I asked him.

"Experience. I've seen a few things out East in other historic sites..." Nathan glanced around and saw a few other people in the area. "Let's not discuss this here."

I couldn't help it. My curiosity was piqued. *Him studying parapsychology aside, how exactly would Nathan know about the lingering effects of magick on a site?* "I think we should discuss all of this with my family. And soon," I said.

Nathan considered that for a moment, and seemed to give in. "Meet me at the Library, Monday afternoon. I managed to make an appointment with your brother at one o'clock. We can talk afterwards."

"Fine." I nodded in agreement.

"Fine," he repeated, and stepped between Cypress and me. "Now, I'm walking you back to your dorm."

Cypress tipped her head over to one side to grin at him. "Trust me Pogue, we're more than capable of seeing ourselves home." She waited a beat. "We're Witches, after all."

"Humor me," he said.

I raised an eyebrow at him. "Why should I do that?"

"It would make *me* feel better." Nathan made an

'after you' gesture.

"Oh for goddess sake." I rolled my eyes. "Come on Cy," I grabbed her arm and marched off.

Nathan fell into step behind us, and to my surprise he did escort us all the way back across campus. He stood at the bottom of the steps at Crowly Hall and waited until we both went inside.

Once the main doors shut behind us I began to laugh. "I can't decide if that was high handed or chivalrous," I said.

"Hmmm..." Cypress stepped into the lobby and shot a grin over her shoulder. "Maybe it was a little of both."

The lobby was deserted, so we settled into the little couch that faced the fireplace. I squinted up at the portrait of Victoria Crowly and considered what we'd seen tonight. *So Victoria had a younger sister...* "I think it's interesting that the only crypt in those cemeteries belongs to Melinda," I said.

"Well, she died young, maybe the husband wanted something more substantial than a tombstone to mark his wife's resting place," Cypress said, resting her head back against the couch. She sighed and closed her eyes.

The lights in the room began to flicker. "The lights are blinking again." I patted Cypress' arm to get her attention.

She snapped her head up from the back of the couch. "It's colder too," Cypress said, her breath showing visibly against the cold air.

Melinda... a female voice drifted through the lobby.

"Did you hear that?' I asked Cy.

Cypress nodded. "You think that's Victoria?"

I stared at the old painting of the founder of our college. "Victoria, we're talking about your sister, Melinda," I said conversationally to the portrait. "We visited her grave tonight." My breath caught when I felt a slight tremble under my backside.

"The couch is shaking." Cypress reached for my hand.

"You've got our attention," I said, focusing on the portrait. "What are you trying to tell us?"

As if in answer, one of the ugly silk flower arrangements tipped over on the mantle with a loud crash.

We both jumped to our feet. I whipped my head around, watching to see what would happen next. But as suddenly as it had began, the lights stopped flickering, and began to burn true. I let out my breath slowly, and the room fell silent.

"Well, that was unexpected," Cypress said. She moved cautiously to the mantle, picking up the vase of fake flowers to put it back in place.

Behind us the front doors opened, and we both jumped nervously as several residents came in together laughing and talking. I patted my chest and let out a nervous laugh. "Sheesh," I managed.

"Let's go up to our room. And talk in private," Cypress said as the girls came into the lobby.

I nodded in agreement. It took everything I had to

calmly say goodnight to the other residents, and walk casually out. Silently, we climbed the stairs to the third floor and made our way down the hall.

I unlocked our door and hit the lights. "Shit!" I gasped, stopping dead in surprise.

Cypress bumped solidly into me. "What?" she said.

At a loss for words I simply pointed. Our dorm room had been rearranged. The bunk beds were now on the opposite wall. The wooden desks stacked on top of each other, and our two desk chairs were balancing precariously on top of the desks, defying gravity.

CHAPTER SEVEN

Once I'd gotten over the surprise, I switched over to record and document mode pretty quickly. I pulled out my camera, and we'd stayed right inside the door while I took several shots from different angles. Cypress stayed beside me and took a video of the bizarre furniture arrangement with her cell phone. The freakiest part of the whole experience happened after I set my camera down. I'd reached for one of the gravity defying chairs and they both tumbled down— right before I could touch them.

I managed to jump back from the crashing chairs in the nick of time. And that too, along with me letting out a loud squeak in surprise, had been captured by Cy's video recording. She emailed me the recording immediately so we'd have a back up. After that there was nothing we could do but clean up and clear out. It took the two of us a couple of hours to put everything back to rights.

Once we finished putting the furniture back in place,

we got to the 'clearing out" portion of the evening. We sat down on the floor and worked a protection spell together. We banished any lingering negativity, and Cypress sprinkled red brick dust along our threshold to repel anything *unwanted* from crossing the threshold of our room, while I arranged empowered, protective crystals along the windowsill to repel ghosts.

Exhausted, we tumbled into bed, and slept hard. We didn't have the opportunity to go over the audio recording we'd made at the cemetery until the next morning. After listening to the tape twice, we were forced to admit that it had yielded nothing but the sorority girls' nervous chatter.

On Monday morning, I printed out my cemetery photos. But I was so busy admiring the way I'd captured the full harvest moon shining through the trees that I had almost missed something important.

In one of my photos, a suspicious blue-green smear of light had showed up. And it seemed to be hovering in mid-air over Melinda Harris Easton's crypt. I went back, double checked everything, making sure it wasn't a printing error or glitch. But the image remained.

I stood at the work counter surrounded by other photography students and tried to stay composed as I studied my newest photos. My intuition was screaming at me again. That sense of unease that I'd first perceived in the library was back. *Ever since they started the construction for the new museum on campus, things had gotten spooky. The discovery of the human remains, and the foundation of that house had obviously opened a paranormal can of worms.*

Forcing myself to stay calm, I put everything I had from my research on the urban legends of the haunting at Crowly Hall, the cemetery photos, and the pictures of our rearranged room in a big manila envelope. I secured the envelope in my favorite magickally themed messenger bag. Large and antique gold, the bag boasted an Ouija Board screen printed on the front.

Somehow, that seemed entirely appropriate.

Cypress was going to meet me for lunch at the Student Union to discuss everything that we knew so far. At noon I walked in to find her standing waiting for me inside the doors of the cafeteria. As usual she was surrounded by guys, and she looked gorgeous. Her dark hair flowed into spiral curls and fell over the shoulders of her ivory shirt. A colorful scarf in reds and oranges was wrapped loosely around her neck. Skinny jeans tucked into brown boots gave her a sort of Boho-chic vibe.

"Hey, Cy." I waved to get her attention, and she smoothly extracted herself from her many admirers. I mentally rolled my eyes, but did not comment.

We selected our food, took our trays over to an out-of-the-way table, and settled in where we would be less likely to be overheard. I draped my black lace shawl over my chair, smoothed the skirt of my layered maxi dress carefully down and sat. The dress was satisfactorily flowing and witchy, in layers of forest green and soft black.

"I'm digging the Dark Mori style you've got going today," Cypress said, gesturing to my dress.

"Compliments on my wardrobe from the campus heartbreaker?" I teased. "I'm honored." I slid the photo free from the envelope in my messenger bag. "You need to see this, Cy," I said quietly, no longer teasing. "I printed this out a bit ago." I handed the photo over.

Cypress sat still, studying the photograph. "Whoa!" Her breath came out in a whoosh as she pointed at the smear of blue-green light. "And it's hovering right over Melinda's crypt."

"Yeah, it is." I spread a paper napkin in my lap to protect my dress. "This was the only cemetery photo that showed any anomalies." I took a bite of my pizza and checked around us to be sure no one was listening.

Cypress met my eyes over the photo. "I made copies of the documentation I'd found on the cemeteries, and Victoria's younger sister," Cypress said. "I verified that Melinda had three surviving children."

"Surviving children?" My pizza seemed to stick in my throat. I tried to wash it down with some soda.

Cypress glanced around too before she answered. "It seems there was a stillbirth shortly before Melinda passed away."

My heart broke a little, and I set the slice down. "Oh damn. Are there any markers at those cemetery plots for an infant?"

"Not that I could find in the cemetery records."

Cypress handed me back the photo. "Or perhaps the tombstone didn't stand up to all the years."

I tucked the photo back in my bag. "So we investigated the campus cemeteries, and I get this weird shot of light floating above Melinda's grave." I drummed my fingers on the table, thinking out loud. "We visit the archeological site and get hit with the heebie-jeebies."

Cypress raised her eyebrows. "Heebie-jeebies? Is that a technical term for a bad reaction to negative vibes?"

"Absolutely," I said. "We run into Pogue—"

"And the whole 'intense magick at the site' theory gets brought up," Cypress said.

"We go back to Crowly Hall afterwards, and it seems like Victoria reacted negatively to us talking about Melinda."

Cypress nodded. "Then we get the big surprise to a rearranged room, with gravity defying chairs."

I reached for my pizza again. "Has anything like that — the furniture reshuffle— ever happened in our dorm before?"

"Actually, it has." Cypress leaned forward resting her elbows on the table. "The book Dr. Meyer gave me mentioned a story from back in the 1970s about some residents of Crowly Hall complaining that their room was constantly being rearranged while they were out."

"Really? It's in the book?"

"Yes," Cypress said. "I marked the page for you with

a pink sticky note."

"Excuse me," a male voice said.

As one, Cypress and I both glanced up. A handsome student stood in front of our table. Tall and muscular, he stood holding a bottle of spring water.

"I noticed you didn't have anything to drink Cypress, so I got this for you." He held out the bottle nervously, and I sat back to see how Cypress handled yet another of her many admirers.

Cypress smiled at him, and I worried for a minute the guy would pass out.

"Thank you..." she trailed off.

"Garret," the guy said.

"Thank you Garret." Cypress took the water and focused on him. Her stack of magickal bangles chimed as they slid down her arm.

Garret blushed and stepped back. "See you around." He grinned and left us to our lunch.

I caught a blush of rosy pink light around her out of my peripheral vision. "Sheesh, Cypress," I said out of the corner of my mouth.

"Cute, isn't he? I think he's in my French class." Cypress rested her chin on her hand and sighed.

I nudged her with my elbow. "If you'd turn down your glamour mojo for a minute, think we could get back to our conversation?"

Cypress winked at me and twisted the top off the bottle. "Right." She took a sip before continuing. "That other 'furniture rearranging incident' from the 1970s?

Most people thought it was a silly prank. But the girls insisted they were telling the truth."

I picked through my side salad as I thought it over. "You don't by any chance know what floor that occurred on, do you?"

"The third floor," Cypress said, and took a bite of her cheeseburger.

I leaned forward. "Oh gods. It wasn't our room, was it?"

Cypress shook her head. "No clue. They never mentioned a room number in the book." She set her burger down, dug into her own book bag, and handed me a big manila envelope. "Here's copies of all the information I gathered. The book from Dr. Meyer, *and* the notes from any paranormal stuff we've experienced so far..."

"Jessica sleepwalking and the flashing lights in the hall?" I asked. "Did you include that as well?"

Cypress nodded. "Yeah, and I made notes on what we experienced last night too. Be sure and share everything with Bran."

"I wish you could come with me," I sighed, tucking her notes into the messenger bag along with mine. "I'm not looking forward to dealing with Nathan Pogue and his attitude again. Even if I'm curious as to what the hell he's really up to."

"Sorry, I can't miss my afternoon class." Cypress smirked at me. "Besides, you can handle yourself just fine around Nathan Pogue."

***

I knocked softly on Bran's office door and waited. When he called out to enter, I took a deep breath, rearranged my lacy shawl over my shoulders, and opened the door. Bran stood behind his desk, and Nathan Pogue sat in a chair. To my surprise, when I walked in the room Nathan rose to his feet.

"Hi Bran," I said cheerfully to my brother. I closed the door behind me and raised an eyebrow at Nathan. He was still standing. "Pogue," I said. My tone was barely this side of polite.

"Ivy," Bran smiled at me and sat back behind his desk. "Nathan has been telling me about some of the accidents at the dig and his concerns."

I took the empty chair and tried not to react to Pogue waiting until after I'd been seated— to sit down himself. "I have some information to share as well," I said to both of them. "Cypress and I have been investigating some paranormal... occurrences I guess you'd call them at Crowly Hall." I pulled the manila envelopes out of my messenger bag and handed them to Bran.

"How long ago did this start?" Bran asked me. He slid the contents of the envelopes out and onto his desk and began to work through them.

"About the same time they began construction for the museum expansion on campus," I said, and proceeded to fill my brother in on everything that had happened at the dorms so far. I was relaying Saturday night's experiences in the lobby, when Nathan interrupted.

"So to be clear," Nathan said, "the disembodied voice, temperature dip, shaking furniture, *and* flashing lights occurred when you and Cypress were discussing Melinda Easton's death?"

"Hang on." I held up a hand. "Let me tell you the rest."

As I explained to Bran and Nathan what Cypress and I had found waiting for us in our dorm room, I pulled out a couple of photos from the stack on my brother's desk. I handed one to each of them. "Sometimes a picture really is worth a thousand words," I said.

Their reactions surprised me.

Bran swore under his breath, and Nathan's eyes went wide. Seeing Nathan's response to the pictures had me reevaluating him, *and* made me a little uneasy.

Bran frowned over the picture. "Ivy, this is serious. You should have told me right away."

"It happened this past Saturday night. Since then Cypress and I have been trying to document this as best we could," I said. "I only printed the photos up this morning."

Bran met my eyes. "You didn't think I would believe you?"

"It wouldn't be the first time someone underestimated me, or didn't take me seriously," I said.

Nathan tilted his head at me as he looked up from the photos. "You kept your cool during a level three phenomena." His eyes met mine. "That's impressive."

I raised my eyebrows. "Dare I ask... what's a level three phenomena?"

"A level one phenomena is often described as things that might be attributed to a seismic incident or a poltergeist situation," Nathan explained.

"Like the shaking couch, and the falling vase," I said.

"Exactly." Nathan shifted fully towards me, getting into his topic. "A level two phenomena is described as phantom footprints or handprints with no apparent human cause." He blew out a breath before continuing. "While a level three phenomena is characterized by items being disturbed in an attempt to get a message, or even a warning across."

My mind raced as I considered what he told me. "Jeepers," I managed.

Bran grinned at the *Scooby Doo* reference. He reached across the desk for my hand. "You and Cypress were very brave." He gave my fingers a squeeze and let me go.

"You've got guts, I'll give you that," Nathan said to me.

"Thanks," I said, cautiously.

Nathan held up a photograph. "Are there any other photos or documentation of the event?"

"Yes. Cypress recorded it on her cell phone."

"She did?" Bran asked.

I took out my cell phone and pulled up the video Cypress had sent me. I handed the phone to Bran. "Hit play," I said, and sat back curious to see my brother's reaction.

Bran watched the short video and flinched at the chairs falling down. I could hear the crashing chairs and my surprised squeak clearly as the video played. "Have you and Cypress taken precautions since this occurred?" he asked.

"We warded the room to keep out any more ghosts." I shrugged. "But once ghosts are in a building can you really *ward* them out of one room in particular?"

"Good question," Bran said, handing the phone to Nathan.

Nathan frowned over the short video. I watched as he replayed it a few times. "You're lucky you didn't get hurt," he said finally.

I picked up Dr. Meyer's book from Bran's desk and flipped to the marked page. "Here, look at this." I handed it to Bran. "The rearranged furniture in Crowly Hall *has* happened before."

While Bran scanned through the marked passage, Nathan held my phone out to me. "At first glance, this would seem like poltergeist activity."

"Well we've got plenty of hormonal girls in the dorm," I said. "I suppose that's possible." I started to take my phone back, but Nathan held on. My eyes flashed up to his.

"I'm not trying to downplay this. Not at all," Nathan said. "I was actually thinking of the true meaning of the word— *angry ghost.*" His eyes stayed on mine, and I wondered at the change in his attitude.

Bran lifted his head up from the book he'd been studying and narrowed his eyes. "Have the other girls in the dorm been talking about any other paranormal activity?"

"Not that I know of." I took the phone back from Nathan and tucked it in my bag. "Well, besides the Freshman Jessica, and her sleepwalking."

"She said something about the *Headmistress*, calling her?" Bran asked, riffling through the notes Cypress had made.

"She did," I said. "But it was the sudden dip in temperature, and the flashing hall lights that made me realize it was more than sleepwalking. It was *creepy* Bran. I think she would've pitched herself right over the steps if Cypress and I hadn't grabbed her."

Nathan shifted in his chair. "Why do you think that?"

"Because," I explained. "She tried to pull away from us before she woke up."

"I want to go over the information you and Cypress have gathered, and share it with Lexie," Bran said.

"Good idea," I said. "Let's get a cop's perspective."

"Are you sure we want to get the police involved? Who's Lexie?" Nathan asked.

Bran tapped the papers into a neat stack on his desk.

"Lexie is my wife. She's a gifted Witch *and* a police officer."

"Oh," was all Nathan could manage.

I made an explosion sound, splaying my fingers wide on each side of my head. "Mind blown," I said, grinning at Nathan's shocked expression.

Bran winked at me and nodded to Nathan. "I pulled several items for you to use in your research. They are waiting for you at the front desk, Nathan."

"Thank you." Recognizing this as a dismissal, Nathan rose to his feet. "I'll let you know if I discover anything."

"You know where to find me," Bran said. "I'll contact you when the rest of the materials you requested are available."

"Ivy, please be careful," Nathan said, glowering down at me for a moment.

Caught off guard, I glanced back up at him. "Sure."

Nathan nodded then hesitated as if there was more to say. Apparently, he decided against it and left the office.

"So, what do you think?" I asked my brother.

"I agree with Nathan. You should be careful until we figure out what is going on." Bran sat back down and scrubbed his hands over his face.

I shook my head. "No, I meant what do you think of Pogue?"

Bran dropped his hands to his desk. "He strikes me as intelligent, in an Ivy League sort of way, but he's a little uptight."

I snorted out a laugh, reaching out to squeeze his hand. "Uptight? I could've said the same thing about you, until you and Lexie got together."

Bran grinned at me. "Yes, well... Love changes people."

***

After the meeting, I managed to avoid Pogue for the next few days. Things had been quiet at Crowly Hall. The cleansing and warding Cypress and I had done to our room seemed to be holding. I kept an ear open but did not hear of any of the girls talking about seeing ghosts or anything paranormal. Instead of making me feel better, the lack of anything else happening made me jumpy, and put me on guard.

I did feel better knowing that Bran and Lexie were checking into the recent paranormal occurrences on campus, while Nathan was supposedly investigating the history of the archeological site. Autumn was still quietly researching Nathan's family line. I told myself to be patient, and started to read up on parapsychology. There were plenty of books on ghosts and hauntings at the University library, so I added that to my college studies.

By the time Thursday rolled around the weather had swung back to hot and sticky. I felt wound up and edgy, almost unable to sit still. I squirmed in my chair, trying to return my focus on my history paper. Thunderstorms had been predicted, and the air seemed dense and heavy. I slid the pentagram pendant my mother had given me back and forth on its silver chain. My face felt hot, a rush of awareness rolled over me, and my heart rate picked up.

Something was coming...

I knew a premonition when I got hit with one. As with all premonitions there was no specific information, only an overwhelming urge to move, to *do* something... to figure out what was wrong.

I wished I could have spoken to my mother about everything that was happening. No one could cut through the bullshit the way Gwen Bishop had. It was funny the way I would miss her so intensely at random times. I felt tears well up in my eyes, and for the millionth time I focused on my mother, reaching out against hope for some type of contact. *Mom, I need you.*

To my surprise, the little framed photo I had of my mother on my desk fell over. I picked up the picture and studied it. The picture had been taken of the two of us at the town's Halloween Ball. I'd dressed up as Glinda the Good Witch, and Mom had worn an elegant red gown. The two of us stood arm and arm. I was puckered up, blowing a kiss at the photographer and Mom was laughing and smiling.

For the first time since she passed away, I heard her voice. *Ivy. Be safe. Trust your instincts, sweetheart.*

I jolted hard. Finally it seemed my mother was

reaching out from the other side! Autumn had confided in me that she'd seen my mother's spirit the night Lexie was attacked, but *I* had not had any sign. For a moment tears swam in my eyes, and my heart raced.

Your intuition is a gift. Trust it. I heard my mother say, plain as day.

It had been almost two years. No dreams, no visions, or messages from my mother. Now hearing her voice had me leaping to my feet.

Cypress snapped her head up from her computer. She pulled the earphones from her head, and studied my face. "What's wrong?" she asked, her eyes glowing amber.

I pressed a hand to my heart. "I was having a premonition, and I heard my mother's voice," I said, my voice catching.

Cypress reached out and put her hand on my arm. "Oh, Ivy." Her eyes glistened with sympathetic tears. "What did she say?"

I examined the little framed picture. "She said to be safe. To trust my instincts." Gently, I replaced the photo to my desk. "Also that my intuition was a gift." I blew out a long ragged breath and tried to compose myself.

Cypress reached out and hugged me. "It's okay," she said, rocking back and forth.

I squeezed her back and let her go. "Cy, I can't shake it. Something's about to happen. My intuition is screaming at me again." The pressure of the premonition was hitting me square in the chest. "I feel it right here." I rubbed the heel of my hand over my heart.

"You've got that look in your eye," Cypress said. "The one that tells me: shit is about to get real."

"Save your work, and power down your computer," I heard myself say. My chest felt tight as I hit 'Save' as well, transferring my current work onto a flash drive. A rain scented gust of wind sent the curtains billowing into our dorm room, as I shut the laptop down.

"I'm on it," Cypress said, doing as I suggested.

"We need to be ready." I tucked my phone in my purse and dropped my memory cards and flash drive in my camera bag. On impulse, I wedged the framed picture of my mom next to my camera and zipped the bag closed. I slung the bag and my purse cross-body, tucking it behind me.

"Is it the coming rain, or something else?" Cypress asked as thunder rumbled.

"Yes to both," I said, and went to check the sky out the window. The early evening sky had turned a sickly dark charcoal color with tinges of green. Clouds rolled and raced, coming in from the northwest. "There's a hell of a storm rolling in." I beckoned Cypress over to the window.

Cypress joined me at the window. The winds grew stronger, and some papers blew off her desk. She pulled her phone out of her pocket, checking her weather app, and frowned. "Wow, we're under a tornado watch *and* a severe thunderstorm warning." She picked up her purse and tucked her phone and flash drive inside. I watched her secure her wallet and glass case inside her huge purse. Cypress zipped it up and slung it over her shoulder, leaving her hands free. As soon as she finished, she slid a little flashlight out of her desk drawer and tucked it in her back pocket.

"The electricity will probably go out again," I said, and sat on the floor to quickly lace up my black converse sneakers. "We lose power whenever there's a storm."

"It's one of the little quirks of living in a building built in the 1850s," Cypress agreed, kicking off her sandals. She laced up her own tennis shoes. She had no sooner stood up when the tornado sirens went off. "Damn it." She grabbed a couple of bed pillows and reached for my hand.

We went out in the corridor. Leann, the Residence Advisor, was working her way down the hall, knocking on doors. Girls were rushing out of their rooms and pushing towards the stairs. "Stay calm. Head for the basement," Leann called out over the blare of the siren and babble of voices.

I stayed at the top of the stairs and did a head count as girls went past me. "I counted ten," I told Leann. "Twelve counting you and me."

"That's everyone on our floor but one," Leann said.

"Let's go." My heart was pounding hard as I followed her down to the main floor. Cypress waited for me at the door to the basement with her pillows. The storm seemed to beat against the Hall, and I tried to stay calm. Cypress and I clattered down the wooden stairs to find the girls all lined up, sitting on the floor with their backs against the old stone walls of the cellar. Many of them held pillows in their laps or had them over their heads.

We went to go sit with the girls from our floor, and I overheard Leann speaking to one of the residents from the first floor. "What do you mean she wouldn't come down to the basement?" Leann sounded pissed.

"I don't think she's ever been through a tornado before. She refused to come down to the basement." Genie tossed up her hands. "Last I saw, Jessica was standing out on the porch watching the storm come in."

"Well go get her!" Leann shouted over the storm.

"I'm not going back up into that!" Genie shot back.

Jessica, again. I felt an inner push and stood. *I had to help.* "I'll go get her."

"Fine." Leann shoved a flashlight at me. "You go up and see if you can get her to come down here."

Cypress jumped to her feet. "Ivy, no!" she yelled. The power went out, sending the basement into utter darkness. A rushing sound, then a loud crack, followed by a *boom* reverberated all the way through the building.

I pulled Leann down to the floor, covering my head with one arm. "Get down!"

"Ivy!" Cypress cried. I felt her hand on my arm, and she dragged Leann and me over against the wall with her.

"Tornado is on the ground!" I shouted to Cypress over the horrible noise from above. I'd been through a tornado once before— the sound they make isn't something that you ever forget.

"Oya be merciful," Cypress prayed to the Orisha of tempests and wind.

Lord and Lady keep us safe, I thought.

We huddled together while the girls screamed, prayed and the whole building shook above us. One horribly long minute later— and everything was still.

I blew out a breath and hugged Cypress tight. "I love you," I said, and meant it.

"Love you back." Cypress squeezed me just as tightly.

Leann clicked on a flashlight. "Everyone okay?" she asked the group.

I saw the lights from several cell phones come on as girls used them as flashlights, and some began to try and text their families.

I cocked my head to one side and listened. It was quiet. The worst of the storm had passed. I blew out a thankful breath— and that relief lasted about five seconds. *Go upstairs! Hurry!* My intuition screamed through my head. "Cypress, we have to go up. We have to hurry," I said, setting my bags aside.

"Jessica?" Cypress stood up, and aimed her flashlight.

Leann, nodded at me. "Oh god! Go! I'll keep

everyone else here."

Cypress grabbed my arm and we rushed up the steps. "This is either the bravest or stupidest thing we've ever done!" she said as we cracked open the door to the main floor.

The double front doors of the Hall were bouncing back and forth, blown open from the storm winds. I couldn't see out past the front porch. The view was restricted by huge leafy branches. I opened the basement door the rest of the way. "Jessica!" I called.

No debris was flying, so we picked our way across the main hall. It was a mess of fallen pictures, broken glass and leaves. When we made it to the main lobby Cypress and I stopped short in the hallway. Part of the lounge's wall was missing. Oddly, the portrait of Victoria Crowly that hung over the mantle was untouched.

I saw a pair of tennis-shoe clad feet sticking out from a pile of furniture and rubble. My stomach heaved.

"Ivy, do you see that?" Cypress gasped, grabbing my arm.

"What?" I yanked my gaze up and discovered that Jessica wasn't alone. A semi-transparent woman stood over Jessica, and she was smiling sadly at us.

CHAPTER EIGHT

For a split second I thought who I was seeing *was* Jessica, but no. *It's someone or something else,* I realized. The fact that I could see right through the red-haired woman didn't frighten me. What scared me was that she appeared to be crying— over Jessica.

"Calamity will continue to fall," she warned us.

"Who are you?" I managed to ask, even though my voice wobbled.

The image of the woman seemed to be across the room one second— and then up and in our faces the next. "Find me. Restore my name." The spirit's image seemed to flicker, but her words sounded clearly over the passing storm. Suddenly the apparition appeared very real as it stood in front of us. "You must uncover the truth!" she said, reaching out.

I flinched when I felt a hand touch my hair. *That was so not cool!* "Hands off, lady," I said, yanking my head away from the ghostly touch.

Beside me, Cypress flinched as well. "How is it

doing that?"

"It's pulling juice from the storm," I said to Cypress out of the side of my mouth. I tried to stand firm and not show fear— but facing off with an unknown entity that was able to *touch me*— that was new for me. I took a deep breath, and stood tall. "You are not welcome here," I said to the spirit.

Cypress took my left hand, raised her right, and pushed power out in front of us like a shield. "Baron Samedi, help your daughters." Cypress held her other hand palm facing out as she stalked confidently forward. "Leave. This. Place!" With each word she spoke, Cypress' voice became deeper, more powerful. And with each word, the apparition was pushed farther away.

I'd never seen Cypress like this. Though Cy played it cool most of the time, she was a very strong, very capable practitioner. Sometimes I forgot how powerful of a magician she was. I moved with her, holding up my free hand in an ancient gesture to ward off evil.

I pushed out with my own magick, adding it to the shield Cypress had conjured. "We banish you from this place!" I said. With a whoosh of sound the spirit was blown back by our magick. It seemed to shoot away, stopping to hover directly over Jessica.

"Get away from her!" Cypress growled at the specter as the two of us moved together, towards the girl on the floor.

The spirit was suddenly less there, less *in* the room.

"You are of the blood." Frowning, she held up her hands as if to placate us. "Sisters, I am not your enemy." She shook her head, as if she were confused. "Not your enemy..." She faded away entirely, a crack of thunder seeming to punctuate her disappearance.

"It's gone," Cypress shuddered, and her voice sounded almost back to normal.

We dropped hands and made our way over to Jessica as quickly as possible. As I climbed over the debris on the floor, my hands started to shake both in reaction, and from pushing out with my magick. "Jessica?" I called loudly, and we started to pull pieces of plaster, glass and furniture off of Jessica.

"Jessica? Cypress said. "Can you hear me?" Cypress bared her teeth, picked up a corner of a love seat and flipped it up and out of the way— by her fingertips.

"Holy crap, Cypress!" I blinked as it rolled past me. *The Loa is still on board...* I realized, and wondered how long Cypress' strength would be enhanced from invoking Baron Samedi.

"What?" Cypress frowned at me.

I tore my eyes away from Cypress to glance back at Jessica's feet, and was torn between screaming, crying, and throwing up. Cypress and I kept working, but Jessica never moved.

"Leann!" I shouted over my shoulder. "Get up here! We need help!"

I heard running and Leann was next to us. "Oh my god!" she gasped, and began to help us shift more debris off Jessica.

I pointed to a large piece of plaster. "Let's get this off." I could hear the rest of the girls rushing up from the basement.

"Jessica?" Leann called to the girl as she grabbed ahold and tried to lift the section with me.

Cypress was trembling, and I saw her stop and throw her head back as the Loa left her completely. She gulped for air, and seemed to remember where she was. She glanced self consciously over her shoulder.

"You okay?" I asked her.

Cypress nodded, then turned to the girls behind us. "Anyone have a cell signal?"

"I'll check the land line. Maybe it still works," Genie answered from out in the hallway.

Leann, Cypress and I wrestled with the large section of plaster. When we pulled it up, there were more girls waiting to help. We continued to try and dig her out with our bare hands, and it took several of us, but finally we were able to move the section aside, uncovering Jessica's face and chest.

"Is she breathing? I don't think she's breathing," I heard myself say.

Cypress reached down. "Jessica?" Her voice was broken.

"I got through to 911, they're coming!" Genie said from behind us.

"I can't find a pulse," Cypress said.

"Let me," Leann said as she stepped in and knelt

down. She dropped her ear to Jessica's chest, and to my surprise she competently started to do CPR. Another girl, a resident named Carrie moved in to help. Cypress and I stepped back out of their way.

"I brought these up for you." Genie handed me my purse and camera bag.

I nodded. "Thanks."

The girls were all gathered together in the hall, and I could hear a few people crying. I stared at Jessica, while Leann and Carrie valiantly tried CPR. Poor Jessica was covered in white dust from plaster. She still wasn't responding or moving.

I knew she never would again.

I clutched Cypress' hand in mine, staring at the spot where the ghost had been, and felt a chill run down my back. I leaned close to Cy's ear, as not to be overheard. *"Calamity will continue to fall*, the entity said. What the hell did she mean?"

"I don't know," Cypress said in a wobbly voice.

I wrapped my arm around her waist and hung on. Now that the energy the Loa had lent her had fully dissipated, I knew my friend would be weak and shaky. "You sure that you're okay?" I asked her.

"I will be." Cypress squared her shoulders, took a deep breath and held it. She blew out her breath slowly.

I started to tremble myself, and my gaze was drawn up to the undamaged, creepy portrait above the mantle. With her black hair formally styled, and her eyes dark and full of secrets; Victoria Crowly gazed coolly down at us all.

***

They moved all of the surviving residents of Crowly Hall directly across the street to the old Hyde Theater. With no cell service it was a chaotic scene. You never realize how dependent you are on your cell phone until a tornado takes out a tower or two.

Word had gone out about a storm fatality on campus at Crowly Hall. The media had descended almost as quickly as the emergency responders. Frightened and concerned parents began to show up to come and pick up their daughters. The girls who were from out of state were taken to the administrator's office where they were able to contact their relatives and let them know they were uninjured.

I sent a psychic message to Great Aunt Faye to inform her that Cypress and I were okay. Bad weather didn't affect psychic abilities, and I was grateful for Aunt Faye's telepathic talents— since she could both receive and send messages. She in turn communicated to me that they had ridden out the storm in the manor's basement and were all fine. Cypress hadn't gotten any word from her family. I had a hunch they were on their way and quietly, I told Cypress that so she wouldn't worry too much.

Leann, Carrie, Cypress and I stayed together. The paramedics had taken over for them once they'd arrived, but Carrie and Leann were devastated at not being able to revive Jessica. Especially Leann, who was a nursing student. The four of us sat in a row at the theater that was lit by a backup generator, talking quietly.

Leann ran a hand through her short blonde hair. "Would you pray with me?" she asked. "Would you mind?"

I stopped fiddling with the gauze the EMTs had wrapped around my hand. Cypress had a few bandages on her hands too. Funny how you never notice cuts and scratches until someone else points it out to you. "Of course I will." I took Leann's hand in mine.

Carrie blinked at Cypress and me. "I didn't know that Witches prayed." She cringed. "I'm sorry. That came out wrong."

Cypress reached over and gave her hand a squeeze. "Yes, of course we do. And no offense taken."

We all joined hands as carefully as we could. Finally Leann spoke up. "Ivy, will you lead us?"

"Ah..." I mentally stumbled for a moment. "Sure." I blew out a breath. *Goddess help me say the right thing.* "Lord and Lady watch over and guide our friend Jessica as she travels to the other side. May she be welcomed by her ancestors and be at peace. Thank you for keeping so many of us safe from harm. Blessed be."

It was silent in the theater for a good twenty seconds after I finished.

Carrie, her eyes red from crying, tried to smile at me.

"Well, that was beautiful. I never thought of it that way. Traveling to the other side and being welcomed by your ancestors..."

Cypress put an arm around her when she sniffled. Carrie and Leann's parents had finally arrived. They jumped up and went to their folks.

"Cypress!" A deep male voice called out.

I watched Cypress' face light up. "Uncle Rene!" The remaining girls and parents jaws dropped open as Cypress ran to her gorgeous uncle. He scooped my friend right up off the floor and held on tight.

I saw Autumn and Cypress' Aunt Marie standing with Rene. I went to my cousin who held out her arms to me. "I'm so glad you are safe." She pressed a kiss to my hair.

I wrapped my arms around her. "One of the girls from our Hall didn't make it," I said, and only *then* did I start to cry.

Cypress dropped her head on her Uncle's broad shoulder. "Ivy and I tried to dig her out. Leann and Carrie even tried CPR... it didn't help."

"Oh, *cher*. I'm so sorry." Rene held her close for a moment, and passed her over to his sister.

Marie rocked her niece from side to side. She met my eyes over Cy's head. "We're taking you girls back to the manor."

I nodded in agreement and let go of Autumn. Rene reached out, cupping my face with one hand. "Ivy." He tugged me towards him. I sniffled and moved into his strong arms for a bear hug.

"Let's get these girls home," Marie said.

Rene escorted us out. We had to walk past Crowly Hall to leave the campus. Even though I felt safe with Rene on one side, and Autumn on my left, I shivered at the much cooler temperatures the passing storm had brought in. With Rene at the center, Cypress and then Marie on the other end, we made quite the human chain.

"Look at us," I said, trying to make them all smile. "Aren't we the fabulous bunch of Witches?" My comment had the desired effect. Everyone chuckled.

However, getting the full view of the front of Crowly Hall made any laughter I'd had wither in my throat. A huge oak tree had come down on top of the columned porch of my dormitory. The tree had snapped, taking out half of the porch and an entire corner of the first floor. Poor Jessica had never stood a chance.

***

Great Aunt Faye, Bran and little Morgan were waiting for us at the Manor. Lexie had been called in and was out working with the rest of the police department. I saw a few downed trees and power lines on the way home, shingles and lots of stripped foliage in the streets, but for the most part the town had been lucky. Aunt Faye fussed over us when we arrived to the darkened manor. She got us fresh clothes, while Marie made us some sandwiches, and my great aunt personally inspected our cuts and scraped hands.

After eating, I sat in the candle-lit family room in Aunt Faye's preferred chair, with Morgan on my lap. He was sound asleep, and even though Bran had offered to take him, I felt better holding the toddler. With the power out, Bran had built a fire and it made the room both cozier and brighter. Merlin stretched out on the hearth rug and basked in the warmth of the flames. Cypress was tucked on the couch between Marie and Rene, while Autumn sat on the floor by me.

Autumn leaned against my leg in support. "So glad you're safe, Shorty," she said, again.

A loud banging on the front door cut off my response. Bran went to answer the door, and to my surprise Nathan Pogue burst into the manor.

"Is Ivy here? Is she okay?" Nathan demanded, grabbing Bran's arm.

"Yes," Bran said. "Calm down, Nathan."

"What about her friend, Cypress?" Nathan said. "I heard there was a fatality at Crowly Hall."

"Ivy and Cypress are both fine," Bran said, trying to reassure him. "A few scrapes but otherwise uninjured." Bran gestured towards the family room.

Nathan swung his head around and gazed at the family all gathered together in the room.

"Come in, Nathan," Bran said.

Nathan seemed to realize he was already in. "Oh." He looked a little embarrassed. "Thank you," he said, and stepped down into the family room. He went directly to me. "Scared me," he said, stopping next to my chair.

"I didn't know you cared." I meant to say that sarcastically, but it came out as more of a question. I felt my face go red, and hoped that the candlelight would cover it.

"Of course, I do," he said.

Bran stood, with his arms crossed over his chest. "Nathan take a seat. Cypress was about to tell us what happened tonight."

Nathan chose the empty chair next to me and sat. Merlin woke up from his spot on the hearth, regarded Nathan with one eye, and went back to sleep.

Cypress cleared her throat. "When the sirens went off we evacuated to the basement of Crowly Hall," she began. She explained to everyone how we'd huddled in the basement, and the moment we'd all realized that Jessica had stayed upstairs. When Cypress reached the part about finding Jessica, she stumbled over her words.

"Go ahead," I said. "Tell them all of it."

Bran dropped his arms to his sides. "What do you mean... tell them *all* of it?"

Cypress grimaced. "I've never *seen* an actual ghost. Standing there— right in front of me before."

"Full body apparition," I said. "She was corporeal one minute and sort of transparent the next."

"You two saw a full body apparition, tonight?" Nathan asked.

After the research I'd done for the past few weeks, I knew what terms to use. "It was sentient. An intelligent style haunt, I'm thinking." I glanced over at Nathan. "It interacted with us."

Marie frowned at her niece. "Was it the campus ghost of Victoria Crowly?"

"No." Cypress shivered. "I wish."

Rene ran a comforting hand down Cypress' arm. "Could it have been Jessica's spirit? Perhaps you saw it leaving the body?"

"No," I cut in quietly, shifting the sleeping Morgan on my lap. "No. It wasn't Jessica. And it *wasn't* Victoria Crowly. This didn't look anything like the portrait hanging in the lobby... This was another spirit. A *different* spirit, or entity. And honestly, she freaked me out."

Autumn gave my leg a supportive squeeze. "You've seen our grandmother's ghost before. She helped us during the search for the grimoire. So why did this frighten you?"

"Because this ghost made me feel so sad, she was crying, *and* I felt her touch my hair," I said.

"I didn't like that she could touch us," Cypress said. "Not one bit."

"I've never seen you whip out your Hoodoo on someone quite like that before," I said to Cypress.

Cypress shrugged. "It was instinct."

"What did you do?" Marie demanded of Cypress.

Cypress straightened her shoulders. "I invoked

Baron Samedi."

Rene raised his eyebrows. "Did he come to your aid?"

"He did," Cypress said, and quietly told the family what we'd done. When she finished, Bran was silent. Autumn and Marie seemed concerned, and Rene crossed his arms over his chest and studied his niece.

Great Aunt Faye tapped her manicured fingernails against the wooden arm of a chair. "Fascinating..." She broke the silence.

"A few days ago the girls shared some of their recent experiences with me," Bran announced to the group. He briefly described what Cypress and I had been encountering at the dorm in the weeks before the storm.

Marie shook her head. "I don't like the way this has been ramping up. The psychic implosion that you all described on the day the remains were found. The surge of negative energy on campus." Marie started to tick points off on her fingers. "Everyone in town knows about the accidents on the archeological dig. Now you've got flashing lights, disembodied voices, shaking furniture, the poltergeist activity in the girl's dormitory, *and* now an interactive, intelligent entity?"

Autumn wrapped her arms around her bent knees. "I'd like to know what the entity looked like."

"Her dress was long," Cypress said. "If I could sketch worth a damn I'd draw you a picture of her."

I closed my eyes and tried to concentrate. "It happened so fast. I only have impressions of her. But I think the sleeves were long too—"

"Her dress was dark," Cypress interjected.

"Yeah, it was," I agreed.

Autumn pursed her lips. "Were the sleeves full, or more slim fitting? What was the shape of the skirt?"

Oh, I got it. "You're trying to figure out *when* she's from by the clothing style?"

Rene grinned at Autumn. "Very clever *cher.*"

Autumn laid a hand on my knee. "Here, let me see," she said. Before I could even blink, she was in my head scanning my recent memories.

I felt the tug on my mind. I shut my eyes, and let her have full access. A few moments later, she patted my knee, signaling that she was finished. I opened my eyes and raised an eyebrow at her. "You're damn good at that now."

Autumn tilted her head towards Cypress. "May I?" she asked.

Cypress held out a hand to Autumn. "Sure, read away."

I watched when Autumn took Cy's hand. Cypress stiffened a bit and then tried to make herself relax. Autumn's eyes shifted back and forth as she read Cypress. Almost like my cousin was speed reading a book.

I checked to see Nathan's reaction. He'd been sitting very still, and I could almost see the wheels spinning in his head as he watched the family.

Autumn shut her eyes, released her breath slowly

and gave Cypress' hand a little squeeze. "All done." Autumn dropped Cy's hand and sat back, rubbing a hand over her chin as she considered what she'd *seen*. "I saw a dark dress with a full skirt. Slim fitting sleeves, an apron maybe..."

"Her hair was red," Cypress spoke up.

I nodded. "And tangled all around her face." Morgan whimpered in his sleep. I automatically rubbed his back, and he quieted.

"Could that have been curls that you saw?" Autumn asked us.

"Maybe," Cypress said.

Bran took a candle over to the desk in the corner and rooted around for a moment. He walked over with a pad of paper. "Here, sketch out your impressions of the clothes."

"I'm no artist." Autumn made a face. "That's Marie's territory."

"Gimme." Marie held out her hand for the pad. Quickly she took the pad. She set it on the coffee table for everyone to see, scooted a pillar candle closer for better light, and began to sketch.

"Dome shape skirt." Autumn gestured with her hands.

Marie nodded and made the skirt fuller. Next she sketched slim sleeves. "Impressions of a neckline?"

"Wide," I said, making a curving motion across my collar bones.

Cypress studied the sketch. "Make the neckline

higher, Aunt Marie."

Marie altered the sketch. "How's this?" she asked, adding curly long hair to the blank faced figure.

My stomach gave a little flip as Marie finished the little sketch. "That's pretty close."

"It is," Cypress agreed.

Aunt Faye cleared her throat to get everyone's attention. "Ivy, would I be correct in saying that neither you nor Cypress has displayed any talent for spirit communication before this incident?"

"No ma'am," Cypress said.

I took my time answering, and decided not to reveal that I'd heard my mother's voice before the tornado had struck. For now I wanted to keep that private. "I've seen Grandma Rose here in the manor twice, once when we found the second part of the grimoire, and when she made her big show with the entire family. But each time it was only because Autumn was holding my hand and lending me some of her power— to help me out."

"Ivy, you said something similar before..." Cypress frowned as she tried to remember. "Like how the storm had lent the spirit power..."

"Yeah," I recalled. "I thought the entity was pulling juice from the storm to manifest." I fell silent. *Was that how mom had gotten her message through? Had she used the power of the approaching storm to communicate with me?*

Nathan, who'd stayed quiet up until now, leaned forward in his chair and took the pad to study the sketch. "That's actually a sound paranormal theory," he said. "Hauntings often are more intense during electric storms."

"That must be how the entity was able to appear to the girls," Aunt Faye said.

"It would make sense that there was a more vivid manifestation," Bran said. "Due to the severity of the storm."

Aunt Faye stood, and we all fell silent. "The question that we need to be asking is why now?" she said. "What happened recently that made this entity appear and with such ominous warnings of calamity?"

I shifted my gaze to Nathan. "You know that this has to be linked to the skeleton that they found on campus a few weeks ago."

"Classically, hauntings do begin when remains have been disturbed," Nathan agreed.

Autumn hugged her knees closer to her chest. "Nathan, you were there the day the archeologist was badly injured on the dig. You witnessed what happened to her."

"Yes," Nathan said, sitting calmly. He seemed unconcerned that the group's focus was now centered on him.

Rene leaned forward and directed his attention to Nathan. "What did happen exactly?"

"The ground caved in under her when she went to remove the human remains from the site. As I told Autumn, it was the strangest thing I'd ever seen, and the injury was serious."

"Why did they remove the remains?" Cypress asked.

"For analysis," Nathan said patiently.

"It's a standard practice," Autumn added.

"I found out this afternoon," Nathan said. "They've determined the bones had been buried for over one hundred years." He focused on me. "I also heard from Dr. Wallis, the head archeologist on the dig, that the M.E. had concluded that the remains were *female*. The approximate age at death being late-twenties to early thirties."

"Female." Autumn nodded at Nathan. "I knew it."

"How would you possibly know that?" I asked her.

"I saw the bones when they brought them into the museum. The shape of the skeleton's pelvis," Autumn explained. "It was more oval shaped— which usually denotes a female."

"Correct." Nathan smiled at Autumn.

"I thought you didn't do bones?" I said to Autumn.

"That's fairly common knowledge," Nathan explained.

"So, female remains," Marie said, trying to get the conversation back on track, "over one hundred years old." Marie tapped her pencil against the sketch. "This type of fashion was typical of the mid 1800s. It's starting to come together."

"I have some other information from the dig site that is important," Nathan said.

Autumn raised an eyebrow. "Oh?"

"There was a high concentration of carbon in the soil. Pieces of charcoal were present," Nathan said.

"Carbon and charcoal?" I asked him.

"Ash," Nathan answered. "From a fire. It means the house probably burned down so that only the stone foundation remained. As the remains were found in the stone cellar, we think that the person— woman may have been trapped. The bones weren't burned so the current theory is that she died from the smoke."

Cypress shuddered. "And she was just *left* there. That's horrible."

Nathan shrugged. "That's the working theory at the moment." He sat back. "Also there were some more pieces found at the site this week," he said. "Utensils, probably silver, a few pewter pieces and an unusual bracelet."

My stomach rolled over. "What kind of bracelet?" I asked him.

"Silver," Nathan said. "With carved coral beads and a crescent moon shaped charm."

"Hmm," Autumn said. "Coral jewelry was common and popular during the 1700s and 1800s."

"I've seen a very similar design before," Nathan said quietly. "That's why I found this so unusual."

"Really?" I said. "Where had you seen the design before?"

"My grandmother owns a piece of jewelry very comparable to it," Nathan said. "The bracelet has been handed down over the generations through the

Osbornes— my mother's side of the family."

I blinked. "The Salem Village, Osbornes?"

"Yes," Nathan said.

My stomach tightened, and my intuition had me blurting out words before I thought it over. "You suspect that the remains found on campus were of a Witch, don't you?"

At my words, everyone in the room went very quiet. Nathan sat back, regarding me seriously. "Yes, I *do* think she was a Witch," he said.

Cypress gasped. "The entity seemed almost offended when we used magick to banish her."

Nathan nodded to Cypress, then turned to me. "Anything else?"

"She called us her *sisters*," I told him, "said we were not her enemy, that we were of *the blood*. Maybe she meant Witch blood?"

Cypress leaned forward. "Is that why she appeared to *us*, because we are Witches?"

"Maybe..." Autumn said, giving me a nudge. "Maybe it was because you were there when they first found her skull, Ivy."

I had to swallow around the fear that had suddenly risen in my throat. "Terrific," I said.

CHAPTER NINE

The next few days passed quickly. The tornado made national news, a few buildings in town had been damaged, and many large trees were uprooted or had broken during the storm. The sounds of chainsaws in the neighborhood and on campus were constant while the town cleaned up. The local meteorologists announced it was an EF2 tornado. There had been several minor injuries, and only one fatality— Jessica. The campus held a candlelight vigil for her, and some reporter from the local paper had gone to Jessica's home town in central Missouri and covered her funeral.

I didn't know how many of the girls from the dorm had attended, but neither Cypress nor I had. We faced enough questions ranging from the curious to the ghoulish from students on campus— as word had gotten out that we'd been the ones to find her. A few days after the storm we were able to retrieve most of our personal items from the dorm, but the building needed structural repair and would not be available to live in for several weeks.

I moved back in the manor temporarily, and Cypress moved back in with Marie to their spacious apartment above the Tattoo Shop. My father and step-mother surprised me and drove down from Iowa to come and visit. My dad had hugged me hard when he'd first arrived, which made me realize that he'd been really worried. They stayed for a few days and then headed west to go and see Holly. I appreciated the effort my father had made, knowing my stepmother was not particularly comfortable with my family's legacy of magick.

I contacted Holly after the storm, thinking perhaps *that's* why she'd told me to be safe... and of course I wanted to share with her that I'd gotten a message from Mom. I never got the chance to tell her. She'd barely spoken to me over the phone. Claimed she was happy to hear that I was okay, but that she couldn't talk as she was busy with her honors society. Surprised and hurt by the brush off, I sat and blinked at my phone for a few moments. I missed her so much, and I wanted to talk to her about hearing mom's voice. It hurt to be disconnected from my twin for so long. At least, it was painful for me.

I woke up surprisingly early on my first Saturday morning after moving back home. I rolled over, blinking at the soft, October light coming in through the curved windows of the turret. Holly and I had taken my mother's old room over before Morgan was born, and I felt closer to my mother here.

A set of celestial fabric cushions decorated the curved window seats within the turret. The room boasted a round sitting area, and the family's books on the Craft were arranged on the far wall. A little loveseat covered in white, and a round, marble topped table stood centered in the space. The table had been used as an altar— my mother's magickal work surface for as long as I could remember.

Even though it had been fun living with Cypress in the dorm... I was relieved to be away from all the paranormal weirdness that had been happening on campus. I was so very happy to be living back at home that it surprised me. Which made me wonder if maybe I should *stay* at the manor and commute to school. I didn't have to move back to Crowly Hall once the repairs were finished.

My bedroom door clicked open, and I saw Merlin's black tail held high as he trotted over to my bed. He jumped up and walked straight across my side to perch on my hip. I rolled over to my back, and he promptly made himself comfortable on my chest. He leaned down and stared into my eyes.

"Hey Merlin," I sighed.

Meow? He reached out and batted the tip of my nose.

I pulled Merlin in for a cuddle, and he allowed it. Sprawling across my chest, he tucked his head against my jaw. He stayed and purred loudly in my ear for a while. When he started to head-butt me, I knew it was time to get up. I staggered to the en-suite bathroom with Merlin trailing behind.

A short time later, with Merlin as my morning escort, I picked up my phone from the nightstand, tucked it in my pocket of my pajama pants and shuffled my way down the back stairs and into the kitchen. I went straight to the fridge and hooked a can of soda. Without a word I plopped into the chair at the kitchen table.

"Ivy!" Morgan waved to me from his high chair. This morning he was eating a cut up banana and Cheerios.

I made the supreme sacrifice and spoke nicely to my nephew. "Hi baby," I said, and proceeded with my morning ritual: chugging the caffeine as fast as humanly possible.

Lexie sat supervising her son's breakfast, wearing baggy gray shorts and a pink t-shirt. She'd left her dark blonde hair down today, and didn't even flinch when I burped. Morgan, on the other hand, clapped and kicked his feet in delight.

"That's better," I said, patting my belly.

"Class," Lexie said with a straight face. "Girl, you have such class."

"You know it," I sighed.

"Why are you up so early?" Lexie asked as she snatched Morgan's toddler cup before he could throw it.

"Beats me."

"Holly called Bran last night," Lexie said casually.

I tried to act nonchalant, but inside all my muscles were locked down tight. "That's interesting. I called her the other day, and she barely even spoke to me." I tried not to be hurt by the news, but it did sting. "At least she's talking to *someone* in the family."

Lexie lifted Morgan out of his high chair and set him on her hip. "I sat up with Bran for hours last night after Holly called. He's still worried about her, and how she's cut herself off from the family for so long."

"Does she hate us so much, then?" I asked Lexie, and to my humiliation my voice shook.

Lexie ran a hand down my arm. "I don't think she *hates* anyone. I think she's punishing herself."

I studied Lexie and Morgan. The toddler was uncharacteristically quiet. "What do you mean?"

"Holly is still frightened about not being able to control her magick, and she wrongly feels responsible for your mother's car accident." Lexie sighed. "As if it was a karmic payback from when she used magick to harm another."

I shook my head. "I think she's ashamed of us. Of the legacy of magick. That's why she chose a school that was clear across the state, and it's why she finds excuses not to come back home."

"No," Lexie said, "you're wrong. Holly isn't ashamed of us— she's terrified *for* us. Because of that she stopped practicing her Craft completely. Leaving William's Ford and going someplace new made her feel safe. It removes any temptation to work magick either with the family, or by herself."

"It almost sounds like you're describing an addict."

Lexie placed her hand on my shoulder. "Bran and I believe that Holly's anxiety over losing control again is very real. Holly's greatest fear is that she will turn completely to the dark path of magick. That she won't be able to stop herself."

It made me flinch in my chair to hear that said out loud. "Do you think that will happen?"

"No, Bran and I don't. But I honestly believe that *fear* is what is driving your twin sister's behavior."

It suddenly, horribly made sense. I put my head in my hands, and my thoughts raced. *No wonder she had refused to come home when we rebound the Blood Moon Grimoire. She was afraid to be around any sort of magick! This explained why she cut me off so quickly whenever I tried to contact her on the astral plane. Why she barely spoke to Autumn, or even to Cypress...*

I rubbed my forehead. "What do we do now?"

"I'm sorry that you're upset. But I think there's something else you should know." Lexie opened a drawer, pulled out a couple of plastic bowls and large orange spoon. She sat Morgan on the floor and he began to play.

"Spoon!" Morgan waved it happily in the air.

Lexie sat down at the table and picked up one of my hands. "Listen to me."

I squeezed her hand back. "I'm listening."

"Bran has discreetly been keeping tabs on Holly

while she's been in Kansas City," Lexie said.

I dropped her hand and did a double take. "Huh?"

"There is a friend of the family, with a connection to the local high council who teaches on Holly's campus. She's befriended Holly and has been keeping an eye on her for the past two years."

"Wait, what?" I shook my head. "Are we talking, like a covert type of magickal surveillance being done on my sister?"

"That's one way to think of it," Lexie said.

I opened my mouth, tried to find the words. And failed.

Lexie tilted her head, her expression serious. "Did you think you were the only one who was upset and worried about Holly?"

The expression on Lexie's face made me feel slightly embarrassed. "Who's been watching over Holly?" I asked. "Do I know them?"

Lexie flipped her hair over her shoulder. "You do. It's Oliver Jacob's daughter, Kara."

I thought back, considering the family connections. Oliver Jacob's son, Kyle, was married to Lexie's cousin, Shannon. "Kyle told me his sister was married and living in Kansas..." *Kansas. As in Kansas City,* I realized.

"Actually Kara is divorced. She uses her married name now, which is White," Lexie said. "Kara is also a High Priestess of her own coven."

"Witches in Kansas, who knew?" I said, trying to

make a joke.

Lexie gave me a withering look. "You know better than anyone that Witches are everywhere," she said. "Not only the William's Ford families— there are plenty of modern day descendants from the earliest lines, all over the country.

"I remember," I said to Lexie. "Bran taught me."

My phone rang and I pulled it out of my pocket and checked the read out. I didn't recognize the number but I suddenly knew who it was anyway. *Speaking of descendants from the earliest lines...* I hit the button. "Bishop's mortuary, you stab 'em— we slab 'em," I said sweetly in the phone.

It was silent on the other end for a solid three seconds.

"Hello Nathan," I said patiently.

"Ivy?"

"Yes?"

"How'd you know it was me?" he said.

"Intuitive, remember?"

"Right," Nathan said, and for once it didn't sound condescending. "That's one of the reasons I was calling. I was wondering if you'd like to help me with my research on the history of the campus' archeological site, today."

I almost dropped my phone in surprise. "You want me to work *with* you?"

"I think it's time to put our heads together," Nathan said. "Pool our resources and talents, so to speak."

"As in two witchy heads are better than one?" I said.

"Exactly," Nathan said. "Why don't you meet me at the University library later this morning. Around 10:30?"

I eyeballed the clock, I had plenty of time to get ready. "Bran has all of my research here at the manor. He made extra copies. I can bring a set along," I offered.

"Perfect, see you then," Nathan said.

I said goodbye and disconnected the call. I glanced up to see Lexie smirking at me. "What?"

"Nathan Pogue? That's the guy from the East Coast?" Lexie said over Morgan, who'd started to sing and beat the hell out of plastic bowls on the floor.

"Yeah."

"Bran said that Pogue was awfully worked up the other night when he burst into the manor looking for you."

"Oh please." I rolled my eyes. "He doesn't even like me." I took another sip from my soda and considered. "So back to Holly," I said, deliberately switching the subject.

Lexie wasn't fooled. She reached across the table and gave my hand another quick squeeze. "What else did you want to know?"

"Tell me more about Kara."

"Kara Jacobs-White is an English professor, and an advisor for the honor society. She keeps a low profile due to her position at the university. They met when

Holly joined the honors program, and Kara has been quietly watching over her ever since."

I sat there, mulling it over. "So Holly has no clue that Kara is actually a Witch, a Priestess, *and* the daughter of a member of our high council?"

"Correct," Lexie said over the racket Morgan was making.

Bran walked into the kitchen. He was wearing old jean shorts and a t-shirt— his yard-work clothes. My brother came directly over and pulled out the chair next to Lexie. "Lexie told you about Holly calling last night." It was a statement, not a question.

"She also filled me in on Kara Jacobs," I said.

"Kara White," Lexie corrected me.

Morgan stopped beating on the bowls and toddled over to my chair. "My Ivy," he said, holding up his arms.

"Here you go." I scooped Morgan up and settled him on my lap.

Bran smiled. "He loves you so much," he said of Morgan.

"It's mutual." I pressed a kiss to my nephew's red curls. *Curls like Holly's,* I realized, and to my surprise, had to work not to cry. "Bran, I wish you would have told me that you were keeping tabs on Holly all this time."

"It was best to keep it as quiet as possible." Bran folded his arms on the table. "Only Oliver, Lexie and I have known. That is, up until today."

I swiped a finger across my heart in an X. "I won't betray your confidence."

Bran reached across the table and squeezed my hand as Lexie had done earlier. "We'll get her back, Ivy. Someday, Holly will come home to us."

***

At 10: 25 I strolled into the campus library, ready to go. Fall was definitely in the air, and in deference to the cooling temperatures I'd worn black jeans, an acid washed gray t-shirt with the phases of the moon printed on it, and topped everything off with a soft and slouchy burgundy cardigan.

I hitched both my messenger bag and camera bag higher on my shoulder and scanned the library. I found Nathan sitting close to the reference desk. He had several books open on the table. He was working on his laptop, and of course he looked amazing. *Damn it.* A faded denim jacket was unbuttoned over a grey shirt and as I watched, he drug a hand through his hair. He scowled at the screen and leaned back down over the books again.

Yup, the scowl worked on him. I straightened my shoulders and reminded myself that I wasn't interested in him. *Nope. Not at all. He's not even my type.* And I managed to maintain that thought until he lifted his head, focused on me, and corners of his mouth curled up.

I don't think I'd ever seen him almost-smile before. He made a come ahead gesture and I walked across the library and pulled out the chair next to him. "Morning," I said, setting my messenger bag on the table.

Nathan raised his eyebrows at my bags. "Hi Ivy," he said after a pause.

"Do you want to get it out of your system," I said, anticipating him, "and make an opening snide comment about my outfit or accessories?"

He cleared his throat against a laugh. "No."

I narrowed my eyes at him. "You're sure?"

"Yes," he said, and maintained a straight face.

"Alright then," I said, and sat down. "Let's get to work."

We dove into the books Bran had secured for him. After an hour or so I started to get twitchy. While Nathan poured over the land deeds, surveyor's maps, and history of the area's surrounding homes and farms, I went through the history of the founders of the University. I dutifully took notes, but was frustrated as what I found was only a slightly more detailed version of the history that Cypress and I had found on the internet.

I propped my elbows on the table and dropped my chin in my hands. "This is getting us nowhere."

Nathan leaned back in his chair and stretched. "Well, we did learn more about Victoria Crowly. She was very devoted to her faith."

"Yeah," I said, "as in apparently she lost a lot of

students trying to convert them to her personal brand of religion." I reached for a book and flipped through the pages. "According to this, her husband George had to use his own personal fortune to keep the school from going under when she drove away students with all her Presbyterian 'devotion'."

Nathan rubbed a hand across his chin. "Sounds like she was recruiting."

"More like proselytizing."

Nathan smirked at me. "That was a fast growing branch of Protestant-ism in the 1800s. I don't imagine *that* information about her losing students is in any of the school's literature about the history of their founder."

"No." I shook my head. "It's all along the lines of 'this brave woman who began a school and a college for young women.' Blah, blah, blah."

"The first west of the Mississippi." Nathan chimed in.

"You know, the church that runs right along the boundaries of the University, is *The First Presbyterian* church."

Nathan started to rifle through some of the surveyor's maps on the table. He pulled one out and considered. "And according to this old map of the grounds from 1900, the cemeteries you and Cypress investigated the other night are listed as belonging to the neighboring First Presbyterian Church." He tapped the map. "I wonder if they bought the land or if it was bequeathed to them?"

I walked around the table to study the map. "You think maybe the Crowly's left them the land?" I said. "It would make sense. Victoria was... let's say *extremely* devoted to her faith, and she had money and pull in the community. I'd check in to that."

Nathan shifted to his laptop and began an internet search. "Hey, your family was a founding family, right?"

"They were."

"Would you happen to know what other older churches are in town?"

"Sure, there's Lutheran and Catholic churches, besides the Presbyterian one right outside of campus. I'm pretty sure the Catholic one is the oldest though."

"Weren't most of the girls, the students at Victoria's school, Catholic?" Nathan asked.

"Probably," I said, leaning a hip against the table. "William's Ford was founded by Spanish and French Traders, most of those were Catholic. It's a safe bet that many of the students were." I wiggled my eyebrows. "But not all of the founding families were Christian, you know."

Nathan actually chuckled. "The Bishops and other magickal families blended in their communities very successfully."

"They kept a low profile, back in the day."

"Unlike their modern descendants."

I glanced up at the big clock on the wall. "Wow, you

lasted longer than I expected." I crossed my arms over my chest. "Almost ninety minutes before there was a sarcastic comment."

"No." Nathan stood up. "I wasn't taking a shot at you. I only meant that your family is very open about their faith. They own a metaphysical shop after all."

I stared at him for a moment. He seemed earnest, and I decided to let that pass. "I'm going to follow my gut, go nose around the stacks and see if it will lead me to any different information."

Nathan pointed to the short stack of books I still had to go through. "Bran left us quite a few. I wouldn't give up yet."

"Ever heard of intuitive versus analytical thinking?" When Nathan stared at me I continued. "Analytical thinking is like a hyper focus on one thing at a time, with no emotion. It may be great for analysis and explaining things to students— but it's one dimensional. On the other hand, intuitive thinking considers *many* things at once, focuses on the bigger picture, and is heart centered."

Nathan studied me for a moment. "You keep on surprising me, Ivy."

I sighed. "I don't know why. I'm an intuitive. I act on hunches even if there is no logical explanation for them. It works for me and I follow my gut."

"Well, you tackle the intuitive end of things and I'll focus on the analytical." Nathan nodded and returned to his research on the land around the campus.

I followed my instincts and started to roam though the local history section of the reference department. Wandering slowly, I let myself tune into the vibe. I soon found myself sitting on the floor looking at a row of books on the bottom shelf. My face felt warm and my heart rate picked up, a sure sign for me that I was onto something.

I ran my fingers across the spines of the reference books, and one fell over. I reached out for it, and found that another book had fallen behind the row. I fished it out and checked the cover. *Life at Crowly Hall*. I flipped it open saw that the book I held in my hands was a reprint from 1940. The original printing date was listed as 1915.

"Hello there," I murmured.

The book was a collection of old journal entries and photographs from the early 1900s. There were architectural drawings of the older buildings on campus, a few old black and white photos of them under construction, and a diagram of the layout of the campus grounds in its earliest stages. I smiled over an old photo of Crowly Hall dated 1912.

I flipped through the book and stopped when I came across a chapter featuring journal entries of a young student of Victoria's. The chapter was set up to provide little anecdotes designed to illustrate the sterling character of Victoria Crowly. Presenting how she had molded these young women into proper, well educated women of society. I rolled my eyes at the phrasing and kept reading.

The book went on to say how the following journal entries, dated 1858, were written by a wayward and headstrong student named Mary Girard: a girl who had eventually been expelled from the school in December of that year— for conduct unbecoming a student. The book claimed that the following entries proved the piety of Mrs. Crowly and would illustrate the devotion she had for her student's safety and of course, their spiritual welfare.

September, 1858. I have made a friend that the Headmistress will not approve of.

The entry began. I crossed my legs, settled in and kept reading.

Mrs. Crowly does not allow her students to walk beyond the borders of the school grounds. If we are to walk outdoors it is always in groups, always supervised, and usually only when we are herded on a daily basis to church. The only thing the Headmistress does seem to approve of is scripture lessons. But these are not the scripture lessons I know.

I went for a walk alone after prayers this afternoon. I was upset and confused after one of the many sermons we had all received. It was warm and stuffy in the hall, and I wanted some air and sunshine. In defiance, I went off alone, and outside of the borders of the campus proper. I found myself some time later at a cabin in a little clearing. When I realized where I was, I was afraid. I'd heard rumors about the local midwife— the woman that some of the people in town whisper is actually a witch.

I know that other girls from the school have gone in secret to see her before. Some to find out their future and others for a love charm. All the girls know that Polly, who was suddenly sent home last year, had gone to the woman in the cabin to try and rid herself of the trouble she had gotten into.

However, I hadn't gone there on purpose. And I was curious. I only wanted to see for myself.

I imagined a haggard old crone would be in residence, but instead I saw a pretty woman with red hair tending her gardens. Her cabin was well maintained with a sturdy stone foundation, and glass windows. It was such a peaceful, and lovely scene that I stood under the trees and watched her for a time. I was startled when she lifted her head from her gardening, and greeted me, even before I had made myself known to her. It was as if she had known that I was there. I was so alarmed that I crossed myself and said a quick prayer to the Holy Virgin for protection.

But the woman was kind. She seemed to know that I was from the school, and she asked me if I was enjoying my lessons. I was shy answering her at first, but she was so gentle and patient with me, that I found myself thinking that surely no woman this pretty, generous and welcoming could be a witch. How ridiculous!

I complimented her on her fine gardens and she smiled as I chattered away about school, and missing my home and family. It was she who suggested I return to the school, and before I left she plucked a small ripe tomato from her garden and gave it to me. Her name is Prudence Thornton. She lives alone in the cabin. I wonder what it would be like to live alone, to be free, without a brother, father or husband controlling your every action.

I will go back to talk to Prudence again as soon as I am able. She was quite frankly the most interesting person I have met since coming to Mrs. Crowly's School for Young Ladies.

"Oh my Goddess," I whispered. "Cabin with a stone foundation, a woman with red hair, rumored to be a Witch. It all fits."

I flipped through the next several pages of the old book. There were two more journal entries from Mary. I jumped to my feet. *I had to show these to Nathan!*

CHAPTER TEN

I rushed to the table where Nathan was still researching and plopped into the chair next to him. "You're not going to believe what I just found!" I waved the book at him.

Nathan jerked his head up. "What?" he said. "What did you find?"

"I think I've identified the remains of the woman at the site." Excited, I reached out and gave Nathan an enthusiastic one-armed hug. "There are three entries in here from a student of the school. They are dated 1858. Let me read you the first."

I began to read out loud and Nathan took notes. When I finished the first entry he gave my arm a friendly squeeze. "This is amazing. A midwife in a nearby cabin. Keep reading. What else does Mary have to say?"

Fascinated, I flipped the page and continued to read to him.

October, 1958. I have visited Prudence several more

times since my last journal entry. She has been busy harvesting and is putting up the fruits from her garden for the coming winter. Today I helped her pull onions and braid them into long ropes to be hung in the stone root cellar under her cabin. Prudence told me that they, along with other root crops, were best harvested under a waning moon.

I also helped her gather the last of her apples from the little orchard behind the cabin. I thought they would be spoiled but Prudence says she wants to get all of her harvest in before the Full Ivy Moon comes.

I stumbled over the words. "Whoa." My eyes met Nathan's over the book, and I felt a little shudder roll down my back. "The Ivy Moon is part of the old Celtic lunar calendar."

"Correct," he said.

"That wouldn't have been common knowledge to most people back in the 1850s. Prudence Thornton is sounding more and more like a practicing Witch."

Nathan made a note on his legal pad. "I'll do a search for the surname Thornton in the 1840s 50s and 60s census and see what else we hit on."

I tried to smile, but it came out a little lopsided. "Kind of a creepy coincidence about the Ivy Moon."

"No such thing as coincidence," Nathan said, tapping on the page. "That was an October journal entry. The Ivy Moon cycle is assigned from September 30 to October 27."

"I know. We're in the Ivy Moon cycle right now." I

cleared my throat. "The moon is waxing too. I call, *Spooky*."

Nathan leaned forward in his chair. "It is a little eerie. An Ivy Moon, and a modern Witch named Ivy at the center of the mystery. I think everything is fated to play out at *this* particular time— for a reason."

I nodded in agreement. "Where was I?" I ran my finger down the page, and found the place I had stopped at. "Got it," I said, continuing to read the second entry from Mary Girard's journal.

I had never heard of a Full Ivy Moon. Then again, Ivy Moon or not, I know that the Harvest Moon was last month, because the people in town had been talking about the bonfire and dance that was going to be held. All the girls at school were excited and hoping that we would be allowed to attend. But Mrs. Crowly forbade it. All we could do was to watch the golden moon rise over the river from the high windows of the school.

I am truly growing to hate Mrs. Crowly. She's so hard on all the girls. With her lessons on deportment, and of course her new religion. She has been trying to pressure me into giving up Catholicism and to become Presbyterian. I was sorely tempted to go to the nearby parish and ask the nuns there to intercede on my behalf with Mrs. Crowly.

I miss her sister, Mrs. Easton. She was so kind, and was my favorite of the three teachers here at the school. I wonder how her husband and sons are faring since her death this past spring. All of the girls were so sad when she passed. I found out that it was Prudence who had acted as midwife to Mrs. Easton. I asked Prudence about it once, and she said the baby had come far too soon, and that Mrs. Easton died of childbed fever a few days later. Mama says men risk their lives in war, and women in childbirth... I suppose that is true.

I got caught when I snuck back to the school tonight. I told Mrs. Crowly that I had gotten lost and that is why I was so late coming in. I had dirty hands, mud caked shoes from helping Prudence in the garden, and I feared I smelled slightly of onions. I do not think the old trout believed me. I shall have to be more careful in the future.

I stopped reading and glanced up at Nathan. "That's the end of the second entry." I blew out my breath and rolled my shoulders at the tension gathering there.

"Go ahead," he said. "I want to hear the rest."

"Okay, here goes..."

November 1858. Mrs. Crowly has sent a disciplinary letter to my parents for conduct unbecoming a young lady at her school.

How I hate that old woman! I wish she would expel me from her school so I can go back home. I'd rather take the veil than stay here another year. The other girls are all whispering about me. Elizabeth started a rumor that I was in a family way and that's why I'd been sneaking off to see the witch in the cabin.

All the other girls laughed when she said that. I was

so angry that I dumped my soup on her in the middle of the dining room. How she screamed when the hot soup poured in her lap! Elizabeth jumped up and pulled my hair in retaliation, and I slapped her face. It took both Mr. and Mrs. Crowly to pull us apart. I am now on probation at the school, not only for fighting but because I have been accused of associating with a woman of loose morals, and for un-Christian like behavior. As punishment, I am to scrub all of the floors in the building every day for a week.

Last week, Mr. Easton came and took his three little boys away from the school. After their mother's death they had been living here, and Mr. Crowly watched over them. Mr. Easton suddenly showed up one afternoon when Mrs. Crowly had gone into town to raise money for her new church she wants to build. The handsome widower bundled those sweet little boys so quickly into his buggy... that it almost looked like they were escaping. I saw the whole thing from my dormitory window. Mr. Crowly embraced his brother-in-law, and as I watched he handed him an envelope. I think it may have had money in it. But Mr. Easton and his sons are well away. No one in William's Ford knows where they may have gone to. Mrs. Crowly flew into an awful rage when she returned and discovered that the boys had left with their father.

I managed to see Prudence again, but I was not able to stay long. I told her what had happened at the school, and she warned me not to come back to her cabin, because it wasn't safe. She said the Crowlys are trying to force her off of her land. That Mrs. Crowly had sent ministers out to Prudence's home and they had tried to bully her into leaving William's Ford. I could see that Prudence was afraid. I hope that all this hasn't happened simply because I began to visit her. I pray that she will be safe. I will be quite sad without visits to her cabin to look forward to. I will miss seeing my friend.

What is happening at this school? The handsome Mr. Easton running away from here with his little sons... Mr. Crowly seems to retreat more every day. He is always locked in his library these days, almost as if he hates his wife and wants to avoid her as much as I do. Now that I think on it, since the death of Mrs. Crowly's sister, the woman has become more fanatical and even harsher. Her daily sermons on piety and proper behavior, not to mention the dangers of the sins of the flesh are sounding more zealous than ever before.

I wonder if Mrs. Crowly blames Prudence Thornton for her sister's death? It might explain her hatred, and why she wants to take Prudence's home from her. I came to this school two years ago for an education, and maybe to be a teacher myself someday. Now all I want is to go home and forget this place.

I have sent a letter to Mama and Papa and told them how unhappy I am. I hope that they will receive it soon. I want to go home.

I sat back and closed the little book. "That's the last

entry from Mary Girard."

"So the local midwife, Prudence, attended Victoria Crowly's sister Melinda Easton." Nathan typed as he spoke. "But the baby was premature, and afterwards Melinda died of complications..."

"And maybe Victoria decided to go on her own personal witch-hunt." I examined the photocopied picture of Victoria's portrait that was lying on top of a nearby stack of papers. "I'm starting to like this old broad less and less," I said, tapping the image.

Nathan held out his hand for the book. "Mary writes that Prudence fears for her land. That's important."

"Why?' I asked.

"Some of the most energetic— active hauntings are often over land disputes, or a need for justice."

"The entity— Prudence spoke of calamity." In my mind's eye I could still see Jessica's feet sticking out from under that pile of rubble. "Do you think Prudence was sad about Jessica?" My stomach lurched at the thought. "Or maybe she was happy that part of Crowly Hall had been destroyed?"

"Let's make a timeline of what we do know so far..." He began to enter in information quickly on his laptop. "In 1853 *The College for Women* was established by Victoria and George Crowly."

"Melinda Harris Easton, Victoria's sister was teaching at the school." I riffled through my own notes, allowing him to catch up on his typing. "From the documentation Cypress found, we know that Melinda

Harris Easton suffered a stillbirth."

Nathan nodded. "Thanks to the entries of Mary Girard's journal we now have confirmed that Prudence Thornton, the local midwife, attended the birth."

"The local midwife with knowledge of the old ways, who lived in a nearby cabin with a *stone foundation*," I said, "like the stone foundation being excavated on campus."

"Melinda died from complications a few days after her child in the spring of 1858 according to the journal," Nathan said, "and by November, Mr. Easton, Melinda's husband, snuck his sons away from Victoria Crowly."

"From the sounds of it," I said, "I'm betting George *helped* him get the boys out of the school."

"Prudence was worried about losing her land," Nathan replied. "Victoria Crowly was— according to Mary Girard— harsher and more unpleasant than ever before. Then in December 1858 Mary Girard was expelled from school for conduct unbecoming."

I drummed my nails on the table. "More likely she was expelled because she dared to make friends with an independent woman who was suspected of being a witch."

Nathan paused in his note taking. "Did you know that in Salem Village a few of the executed women in 1692 were midwives themselves?"

"No," I answered. "No, I had no idea."

Nathan went back to his notes. "The local M.E.

concluded that the remains found here on campus within the foundation of the house, were over one hundred years old. They belonged to a female, aged mid twenties to early thirties," Nathan said.

I nodded. Things were starting to fall together, but I still wondered. "How do you suppose she— Prudence, I mean, ended up dying in the cellar of the cabin?"

Nathan stopped typing and met my eyes. "Remember what I said the night of the tornado? According to the soil analysis at the dig— the high amount of carbon that was present— we can speculate that the cabin burned down."

"And they *left* her there?" I shuddered. "By the gods, you don't think the locals descended on Prudence with pitchforks and torches, do you?"

"I hope not," he said, and gave my fingers a reassuring squeeze. "Fires were common. Maybe it was simply a chimney fire that got out of control, and Prudence was trapped in the cellar and overcome by smoke."

"What a horrible way to die," I said. "So Prudence died in the fire and her cabin was gone. Did the Crowlys simply take her land afterwards?"

Nathan pulled out a surveyors map dated 1859 and spread it across the table for me. "Look here," he said. He pointed to the area marked as Crowly Hall. "Here's Crowly Hall." He ran his finger clear across the map to an area marked as *The Orchard.*

"Wait." I pounced on the book and flipped back to

the journal pages. "Mary Girard wrote that she helped Prudence gather apples from a *little orchard* behind the cabin!"

Nathan took out a second surveyors map and spread it over the first. "This map is more modern, but I have a hunch. This could be very illuminating." He smiled at me over that.

Nathan held the maps up to the light, aligning Crowly Hall on the papers. I pulled my camera free of its bag and ducked under to stand in the middle of his arms to better see the maps.

"Don't be shy," Nathan said.

"Don't worry, I'm not." I ignored him. As the light from the ceiling lights showed through the papers, I could clearly see most of the current buildings on campus. I found the modern history museum, and discovered that *The Orchard* area marked in 1859, was adjacent to the current history building, and smack in the center of what was planned to be the expanded museum— the current site of the archeological dig.

"Nathan," I said, trying to stay calm, "when they first started to clear the land for the construction, they bulldozed a stand of really old *apple* trees."

"Are you sure?" he asked.

"Positive," I said. "Cypress and I stood there taking in the torn down trees, and were sad because that meant no more apples." I shook my head. "Can you hold the maps up a little higher? I want to document this."

"Go ahead," Nathan said, his lips very close to my

ear.

I focused my lens, shifted my stance, and took several pictures. I stopped, and without thinking about it leaned back against Nathan as we continued to study the maps together. "We need to call Bran. He's going to want to see these," I said as I continued to stare up at the images.

"Agreed." Nathan's voice was husky as he lowered the maps, and I found myself surrounded by his arms.

The huskiness of his voice should have been my first clue that the energy surrounding us had changed. Realization dawned a few seconds too late, and I felt my solar plexus tighten in reaction. I turned slowly around to face him, and neither one of us moved. For a few moments we stared silently at each other. I swallowed past a lump in my throat. "Well," I managed, wondering if he was about to kiss me.

Nathan let go of one side of the maps, opening his arms. "I should call the lead archeologist, and Dr. Meyer as well." He stepped back, slowly. I stepped away too, and he carefully set the large maps back on the table.

I did my best to act casual, as if I hadn't been chest to chest with him and staring into his eyes a few seconds ago. "Hold the reference book open for me, will ya?" I said, doing my best to sound nonchalant. "I want to take some photos."

"I can make photocopies of the book pages for you," Nathan said.

"I'll want photos anyway," I argued. "It'll only take me a few moments. I'm not going for portraits."

"I was going to ask you to take more photos of the maps, anyway," Nathan said, turning a page over for me. "We shouldn't put the old surveyors map through a photo copier."

"Good point," I said, pushing my sweater's sleeves up to my elbows.

"And I'll want my own copies," Nathan said.

"Me too," I agreed. "Once we call in Bran, Dr. Meyer and the lead archeologist, they are probably going to want to take all today's research," I said, gesturing to the work on the table.

"Most likely," Nathan agreed.

"I figured," I said. Then I got to work taking photos as quickly as possible.

A short time later, I dug in my purse, got some change, and walked over to the copy machine with him. Nathan pulled some quarters out of his own pockets, and I fed the change slot. He started the machine to print out the section of the reference book with the reproduced journal pages.

"So, it's not quite the kind, maternal image of the school's founder that we've all been told about," I said over the copy machine.

"They did a hell of a PR campaign to soften Victoria Crowly's image over the years," Nathan said, making three neat stacks of pages.

Once he was done we went back to our table. I put

my camera back in the bag, tucked away all of my own personal research, and set my phone on the table in front of me. "Why don't you contact Dr. Meyer and your head archeologist?" I suggested as he finished up straightening his own research. "And I'll call Bran."

Nathan set his hand gently over mine where it rested on the table. "Even though this will not be a popular theory, with the suits at the college, it is an *important* discovery none the less."

"Oh, jeez." I frowned. "Paranormal issues aside, I hadn't thought about that."

"Well, let them bitch all they want," Nathan said. "This is a solid lead on identifying the human remains, dating the cabin *and* uncovering some of the forgotten history of William's Ford."

I flipped my hand over and threaded my fingers through his. "Will this discovery help you with your Master's degree?"

"It sure the hell won't hurt," Nathan chuckled.

"I don't think we should mention any of the paranormal incidents to the archeologist," I said. "Dr. Meyer, we should tell him in private. He's a ghost enthusiast and a historian. He would *love* that."

Nathan smiled over the idea. "Yeah, considering he wrote a book about the campus hauntings."

"Maybe we should let my brother Bran tell him?" I said. "He'd probably listen to Bran, take him more seriously."

"You know he'll want to interview both you and

Cypress about your experiences," Nathan pointed out.

I hunched my shoulders. "Aw man, I hadn't thought about that."

Nathan chuckled and released my hand. "I'm glad we were able to work together on this, Ivy."

"So am I," I said, and then I had a moment while he began to make his calls to realize that I actually *was* glad.

***

I'd never seen academics lose their shit over something before. It was sort of cute. I stood back and let Nathan explain what we'd found to the group. Bran was quiet but excited over what Nathan and I had uncovered. The Archeologist, Dr. Wallis, was thrilled with Nathan's initiative and the information we'd put together, and Dr. Meyer? Well I thought for a while he might actually pass out from excitement.

A few hours later, the surveyor's maps and the reference book were safely under Bran's care. Dr. Wallis had left, and Bran invited Dr. Meyer into his office for a private conversation. Bran gave me a significant look as he ushered the older man in, and I knew he was about to share all of the paranormal information and documentation that Cypress and I had gathered with the historian.

I slipped my camera and messenger bag straps over my shoulder. "Let's take a walk," I said impulsively to

Nathan, "I need to get outside for a while.

"Get some fresh air," Nathan said, "sounds good."

As soon as we stepped outside of the library I inhaled, deeply. The crisp October air was slightly spicy and smelled of leaves and chrysanthemums. "Better." I faced the sun and stretched my arms over my head. "Much better."

"It's a nice day," Nathan commented as he stood beside me.

"It's a great day," I said, plucking my sunglasses from my bag, and stuck them on my nose. "We kicked ass in there."

"We did." He lifted his face to the sunshine as well. "You want to get lunch, or something?" Nathan asked, casually.

I pressed a hand to my heart, as if overcome. "Why Mr. Pogue, did you just ask me out?"

"I guess I did."

"I'm a little overcome by the sheer suave-ness of your invitation," I said, tipping my sunglasses down to peer at him from over the tops. "You'll have to give me a minute."

Nathan snorted out a laugh. "Smart ass."

"Ah, you're finally catching on!"

I pushed my glasses back up my nose, delighted to discover that there was a lopsided grin on his face. "You have a nice smile."

Ah... thanks." Nathan seemed a little thrown by my compliment.

I shook my hair back and looped my arm through his. "You're so serious all of the time Nathan. You should lighten up, learn to smile a little more." I sighed, happy to be outside on such a pretty fall day. "Let's walk."

"Where are we walking to?" Nathan asked as he strolled along with me.

"I don't know yet. I think there's somewhere we need to be." I patted his arm. "Trust me, and let's see where we end up."

"Intuitive versus analytical walking?" Nathan said.

"Did you crack a joke?"

He grinned down at me. "Only lightening things up."

"Let's follow the vibes," I said, ambling along. I was starting to feel pulled in a specific direction, so I followed my gut. I knew as soon as I saw the building — where we needed to go.

We stopped in front of Crowly Hall. The building was still closed and unavailable to live in, but the repairs were underway. Scaffolds ranged along the front of the old building, and a new massive column had been put in place, replacing the one that had been taken out by the tree. I could see that repair work had begun on the brick exterior. Large stacks of bricks were neatly placed and waiting at one corner of the building.

Nathan shielded his eyes with his hand. "They started to rebuild the porch."

I stood staring up at the old building and noticed movement in one of the windows on the ground floor.

"Look at the far left window on the ground floor," I said urgently. My heart began to beat faster as I saw someone walk back and forth in front of the window.

"I thought the building was closed for repairs."

"It *is* closed," I said, "supposedly locked up tight."

"Who the hell is in there?" Nathan asked.

"I'm sure as hell going to find out!" I took off at a run. I moved around the building, skidding to a halt at the back door. "Let's see if my keys still work." Before I could pull the keys free— there was a solid click. The door swung open, and I stepped back in surprise.

"Did *you* do that?" Nathan asked, stopping beside me.

"No, I didn't," I said. "It's like somebody or some thing *wants* us to come inside." As soon as the words left my mouth the door swung open even further. The sound of a woman crying drifted out to us.

Nathan shot an arm out as if to block me. "Don't!" he hissed. "I don't like this. I feel like we're being lured into the building."

"Like Jessica was *lured* out of her dorm room to sleepwalk down the hall and towards the stairs?" I said what I was thinking. As we stood there the crying grew louder, more desperate. "What's the play?" I asked him, quietly.

"We can't go in there unprepared and energetically unprotected."

Mom used to always say: go forward with awareness. I recalled. "I have a few things on me that might help," I said, pulling the large silver pentagram pendant out from underneath my t-shirt. "I have magickal protection— my mother gave me this amulet." I let it rest on my shirt. "It's powerful, and has worked well in the past."

"I have an amulet too," Nathan said, and pulled a triquetra circle amulet out from under his own shirt. "My father gave me this." The Celtic triple knot interlaced with a circle had a soft silver sheen, and was tied onto a practical leather cord.

"I've been carrying some protective crystals," I said, and unzipped my soft sided camera bag. I pulled the camera free and looped it around my neck. The trio of protective stones I'd put in weeks ago were still there. "Take the tiger's eye, I'll take the other two." I handed it to him and put the hematite and snowflake obsidian in my front pocket.

"Let me see if there are any herbs we can use." Nathan pulled a pocket knife out of his jeans, stepped back and began to scan the immediate surrounding landscape at the back of the hall. "Wait for me," he cautioned.

"I will," I said, folding the camera bag flat and putting it in the roomy messenger bag. I switched to wearing the long strap to cross-body, and tucked the bag behind me, leaving my hands free. I checked my camera, and prepared myself. *Maybe it was only a student skulking around inside the dorm, or maybe it was something less corporeal.* Either way, Nathan was right. It was better to be prepared.

Nathan handed me a long trailing piece of green ivy, cut from the landscaped beds at the back of the Hall. "Ivy is a protective plant, it shields from negative influences."

I blinked at him for a moment. "I would have never pegged you for a magickal herbalist, Pogue."

He lifted his brow. "Herbalism is a classic part of any Witch's repertoire. Besides, this seemed pretty appropriate." He held out his left hand. "Here, tie it around my wrist."

"The protection magick would probably work better if we maintain body contact," I said, and tied it on him. "Here, do mine." Finished, I held up my right hand to him.

"Good idea," Nathan said, knotting it tight. He took my right hand with his left. "By the power of the old ivy green," he chanted quietly, "protected from harm and energetic attack we both shall be."

I felt a tingle rush up from where our hands were joined. The energy was warm and ran straight to the back of my neck. "By the powers of earth, air, fire and water; Lord and Lady protect your son and daughter," I said, adding to the protective charm.

"So mote it be," we said together.

I nodded to him, and he gave my hand a squeeze. Without another word we stepped up into the Hall, still holding hands.

CHAPTER ELEVEN

The door slammed shut behind us as soon as we cleared it. I couldn't help but jump a little in reaction. I huffed out a breath. "*Oooh* a slamming door. How cliché," I said to whatever was listening.

Nathan stared at me open-mouthed. "Maybe now isn't the best time to be snarky."

I shifted the camera strap around my neck. "Snarky is my default mode."

"We need to keep our voices down," Nathan warned.

"Yeah, we don't want to get busted by campus security," I agreed. "Come on, follow me." My intuition was pulling towards the lounge. I psyched myself up, led him quietly down the hall and turned right.

We stopped together in the doorway. I could see the once missing walls had been reframed and new drywall was screwed in place— still waiting to be taped. The large room was empty except a metal step ladder, several rolls of the white mesh material for taping over the seams, and a few big buckets of joint compound for the drywall.

Nathan pointed with his free hand. "The empty spot over the fireplace? Is that where Victoria Crowly's portrait used to hang?"

"Yeah," I said, frowning at the darker rectangular shape on the wall. "I heard that the painting is in storage for now." I stayed in the doorway and did not enter. As we stood there, the sound of weeping drifted softly through the lounge.

"Do you hear that?" Nathan asked. "The sound of a woman crying."

"I do. Maybe it's Victoria, crying over her sister's death." As soon as the words left my mouth, the ladder fell over with a loud crash. I cringed, took a step back and moved farther out into the main foyer.

Nathan moved our clasped hands so that the back of his brushed against my side. Keeping contact, he let go of my fingers and ran his arm around my waist instead. "Camera," he breathed in my ear and gave my waist a friendly squeeze. "The last time you spoke of Melinda's death," his voice was louder now, and directed to the room, "a vase was knocked over."

"That's right," I said, taking hold of my camera and keeping an eye out for anything else that might fall over.

"This room is where the student died?" Nathan asked as the crying continued.

"It is." I nodded, purposefully averting my eyes away from the lounge floor.

"Where exactly did you see the entity that night? Point out where she manifested."

"At first Cypress and I saw her by the pile of rubble. She sort of zoomed over and was right up in our faces. About where we are standing now." My voice was husky and I cleared my throat. "After we tried to banish her, she was hovering, sort of, a little to the right of the fireplace, over Jessica's body."

The sound of the weeping faded and the Hall was hushed. The only thing I could hear in the quiet was my own breathing, and Nathan's.

"I want to try something," Nathan whispered to me.

I lifted the camera and brought the room into focus. "Go ahead."

"Melinda," he called loudly. As if in answer, there was a loud thump from somewhere above us.

The sound of footsteps began to echo in the empty building. I cocked my head to one side and listened. "Is someone— a physical person someone— upstairs?" I whispered, and the sound stopped.

Nathan moved back, pulling me with him further into the foyer. He seemed suddenly very interested in the main staircase. "Nothing corporeal has been up and down those stairs for a while," he said quietly.

"Okay, I'll play Watson to your Holmes," I said softly. "How'd you deduce that?"

Nathan pointed. "The textbooks that were abandoned — see how the books lying on the staircase are covered in drywall dust?"

I moved closer to the steps to see for myself. "Yeah, everything has white dust on it, but there are no smudges or marks on the wooden stairs." I framed the staircase and the books in, and took several photos. "I read that Parapsychologists sometimes sprinkle flour or powder over the floor to see if anything smudges it or disturbs it when they do investigations."

"Exactly," Nathan said as I lowered my camera. "The floor in the foyer and the lounge itself has footprints— ours, and the workmen's. But the drywall dust on the stairs is unmarked."

The sound of footsteps above us started up again. I held my breath and waited. But as before, they faded away. I shuddered in reaction.

Nathan pulled me closer so I was snugged up tight against his side. "Let's go back for a closer study of the lounge," he suggested.

I balked. "You go ahead, I'm staying out here in the foyer."

"Are you okay being back in your dorm?" he asked.

I nodded, but stayed where I was. "It's sad to see the spot where Jessica died."

"Are you *sensing* anything?"

"Not with my psychic abilities, no. I'm not an empath like my twin," I said. "Holly would be able to pick up on any lingering emotions in the room, not me."

Nathan's eyes popped wide. "God, you have a twin? There are *two* of you?"

"Holly is my *fraternal* twin," I said, rolling my eyes

at him. "She's older than me by five minutes." When he continued to stare I elbowed him in the ribs. "Relax, there's only one of me, Pogue."

Nathan stood, frowning down at me. "And your mother named you two Holly and Ivy?"

"We were born on the Winter Solstice. She'd always said it seemed appropriate."

"Why haven't I met your sister? No one in your family ever spoke of a twin. Where is she?"

I sighed. "She abjured her Craft and moved away to the other side of the state to go to school, two years ago."

"Why would she give up her Craft?"

"Long story short?" I stepped away from him, no longer wanting his arm around my waist. "A few weeks before my mother died, Holly lost control of her magick. And it was pretty bad."

"She used her powers to harm?" Nathan's voice was soft as he stepped closer to me, his expression intense.

"Yes, she did," I said, dragging a hand through my hair. "Not that she wasn't provoked... but yeah, she attacked another girl with her powers."

Nathan reached out and rested his hand on my shoulder. He stayed silent, waiting for me to continue.

"She was working on making amends and gaining better control of her magick, when our mom died," I said.

"Did that set her over the edge? Was she worse after your mother's death?" Nathan's question sounded unemotional, as if we were casually discussing the weather.

"No, actually it shut her down. She stopped practicing altogether." I took a breath and tried to steady myself. "Then my sister moved away and went to another school clear across the state. These days, Holly finds excuses not to come home. She rarely talks to us anymore. I haven't seen my twin since last year."

"Ivy, I have two sisters. They both live in Massachusetts with their families," Nathan said. "I don't see them for months at a time now that I'm going to school here. We're still a family no matter where we live." He patted my shoulder. "Don't you think you're overreacting?"

"You don't understand," I said, my voice rising along with my frustration. "Holly was my other half— I grew up learning magick with her! We practiced together. When my sister abjured her Craft, she basically cut off half of my magick!"

"You were dependent on her." He stared down at me, almost in a clinical way, and that *really* pissed me off.

"Thanks for that brilliant insight, Captain Obvious," I snapped, jerking my shoulder out from under his hand. "I was, and still *am* dependent on her!"

Nathan held up his hands, placating. "Easy, keep your voice down."

I suddenly remembered where we were, skulking around in an off-limits, haunted and historic building. I closed my eyes, trying to compose myself. "Truth is?

My magick *sucks* without my twin by my side."

"Why would you think that?"

I growled in frustration. "Because..." I flung a hand out towards the lounge, and a roll of drywall tape shot towards me. I snatched it out of the air and waved it in his face. "Despite my telekinesis, my spell casting still works best when I work *with* another practitioner."

"The amount of control you have over your telekinetic ability is impressive," Nathan said in a serious tone. "Being able to manipulate inanimate objects is rare."

I set the tape down on the floor. "Yeah it's a swell party trick," I groused, pointing at the roll and then aiming my finger towards the lounge. The tape rolled away, curving into the lounge. It came to a neat stop next to a five gallon bucket of compound.

"Ivy," Nathan said, "most Witches would give anything to be able to do what you dismiss as a 'swell party trick'."

I felt a ripple of air roll over me. It blew hard at my back, and my hair shot into my face. I shoved it out of my eyes and spun around to see where the draft was coming from. "What the hell?" I said, watching as Nathan's hair waved away from his face.

Nathan reached out, winding an arm around my waist. "Here we go," he said in a grim tone of voice, squinting up the dark stairs. "We should stay together," he said, and pulled me tight along his right side.

I shivered at the sudden cold. "What's happening?"

"The barometric pressure dropped," Nathan said out of the corner of his mouth.

"Show time?" I asked, half thrilled— half terrified.

"Get your camera ready," he said as footsteps sounded loudly, again. "It's coming down the stairs."

"You don't have to tell me twice." I quickly tucked my left foot around his right. I leaned my shoulder against him so that we maintained even more body contact, leaving my hands free.

"Good idea," Nathan said. Keeping his eyes on the staircase, he lifted his arm over my head and dug his cell phone out of his pocket. He switched the phone over to video record and aimed it up the steps.

We stood hip to thigh. "Will you share energy with me if necessary?" I whispered, raising up my camera as well, and focusing towards the second floor landing.

"Of course," he said, and I felt his body stiffen in surprise. "There she is."

I don't know what I expected, but seeing a wispy, black and white version of Victoria Crowly floating on the second floor landing— through my viewfinder— was *not* it. "Shit." I managed to snap a few pictures, and I lowered the camera so I could see her with my own eyes.

Victoria Crowly's ghost seemed almost illuminated. I could see her face, arms and upper body, but the rest of her sort of disappeared from the knees down. Her brows were lowered, her mouth was set in harsh, and unyielding lines. Her hair was styled as in her portrait, and I could see a lace collar and cameo at her throat. That little smile on her face that had always creeped me out from the painting was gone— and replaced by a scowl.

Nathan's breath left him in a rush. "Wow," he murmured as the spirit moved farther down the stairs.

I saw a soft glow out of the corner of my eye and glanced over to see that Nathan's triquetra circle was gleaming. The pentagram amulet around my neck was also shining with a soft white light, but that wasn't all. The bands of ivy encircling our wrists were both illuminated too. "Our protective amulets and the charmed ivy are reacting to the ghost," I whispered. "Nathan, they're glowing brighter the nearer the ghost gets to us."

"That's close enough," Nathan said. He shoved his phone at me. I grabbed it right before he rolled his wrists and pushed out with his hands in one smooth gesture. I felt a thud in my chest as he manipulated the energy around us. A ring of blue light shimmered to life across the dusty tile floor, circling clockwise around our feet. "Stay in the protective circle," Nathan warned me.

"Witches!" Victoria seemed to pause. "Get out of my house!" she hissed.

"This isn't your house," I said in a shaking voice. I handed Nathan back his phone. "Not anymore." I tried to sound brave, and raised my camera to take a few more pictures.

"Crowly Hall is a dormitory," Nathan said, lifting the

phone up again so he could continue to record. "The school you started is a university now."

A spectral wind continued to flutter my hair back from my face, as the ghost floated to the bottom of the stairs. *That's not good,* I thought, letting my camera rest against my chest. *If we're in a magick circle the wind— or whatever it was— shouldn't be able to touch us.* Concentrating, I took a deep breath and lifted my right foot a few inches. I stomped my foot down, and pushed out with my own power. The circle blew out a tiny bit wider, only a few more inches, but it became a deeper shade of blue.

Nathan leaned in closer along my side. "Nice job," he said appreciatively.

"I'm just glad it worked," I said. That 'wind' still seemed to make Victoria Crowly's hair and clothes flutter... But now, safe within the strengthened boundaries of our protective circle, it was calm.

"Victoria." Nathan's voice sounded composed and reasonable. "Why are you still here? Are you looking for Melinda?"

"Melinda." Victoria's voice echoed through the foyer. "Where is Melinda?"

"She's gone," Nathan said.

"But Prudence was here," I said, deliberately. "Do you remember Prudence?"

The ghost whipped her head around and made a horrible face at me. "Oh *shit*," I said, as her face seemed to stretch down, and her mouth became impossibly long.

"Son-of-a—" Nathan began.

The ghost cut him off, letting out an enraged wail. "Get out!" she shrieked. The force of her voice seemed to shake the walls.

"I banish you from this place!" I shouted at the ghost. "By the powers of earth, air, fire and water, I banish you!"

Apparently that pissed her off, because the books that had been abandoned on the stairs shot out in all directions. "No!" I yelled. Instinctively I threw up my hands and pushed out with whatever magick I had. It worked. None of the flying books were able to penetrate the energetic circle that surrounded us.

"You are not welcome here any longer," Nathan said, sounding tough as nails. "Go, find peace and walk no more."

The ghost blew past us in to the lounge, and as she roared past several more books bounced off our shield and fell to the floor. Nathan and I turned as one, only to see her disappear as she shot through the spot on the wall where her portrait used to hang.

Before I could blink or catch my breath, another spirit shimmered to life within the open doorway of the lounge. I saw impressions only— red hair, a sad oval face. But I *knew*. "That's her," I whispered to Nathan. "It's Prudence."

"The same spirit you saw the night of the tornado?" Nathan said, aiming his phone at the new spirit.

"Sister." The feminine voice was husky and low. The rough shape began to fill in. Becoming more defined—more real. She bowed her head to me, and then to Nathan. "Brother."

"Are you Prudence Thornton?" Nathan asked the ghost.

"I am," she said, holding out her hands in supplication. "They took my property, my orchard."

"I'm so sorry," was the only thing I could think to say. I fumbled with my camera and tried for a few pictures.

"Burned my cabin, and left me to die," Prudence cried. "Even my magick couldn't stop them."

"Was it the Crowlys?" Nathan asked. "Did they want your land?"

"It was her!" Prudence's voice became stronger as she pointed to where Victoria's portrait was usually displayed. "It was always her."

"Victoria Crowly?" I wanted to clarify. "She came after you because of her sister's death? Because of Melinda?" When Prudence inclined her head, I took that for a *yes*.

Her lips lifted in a sad smile. "Listen well— before the Ivy Moon begins to wane, calamity will fall unless you restore my name."

"We're working on it," Nathan said. "Prudence, I promise you."

Prudence's image grew brighter. "In the quiet place where she rests, surrounded by an iron gate; bind her with blood to protect another sister from her rage and hate," she said, and began to fade away.

"Rhymes," I said, shaking my head at the rough human shape that was left in the doorway. "Why do they *always* do the rhyming thing?"

I clearly heard what sounded like a little laugh from Prudence. "Sister, ask the other to help you."

And then, she was gone. "Other?" I slanted my eyes to Nathan.

Nathan seemed as confused as I felt. "What *other*?" he said, tapping the screen and ending his recording.

I saw movement in the hallway to our right. A shadowy figure moved towards us, and I didn't even think— I reacted. I pointed at one of the books at my feet and sent it flying towards the movement in the door. The book went soaring like a missile towards the 'head' of whatever *thing* might be there.

"Ivy!" Nathan yelled.

To my horror, I recognized Dr. Meyer at the last second. "Stop!" I shouted, and the book froze in mid-air only a few inches from the man's face.

"Amazing," Dr. Meyer murmured. He reached out carefully and touched the hovering book.

I rolled my fingers towards my palm and turned my wrist. The book zipped right towards me and I snagged it. "Dr. Meyer—" I began.

"Hal," he said, staring at me. "I think under the circumstances you can call me Hal."

Mortified, and frightened at what he would do, I

fumbled for the right words. "Let me try and explain," I begged.

"Explain what? The ghost you were communicating with? The protective circle you and Mr. Pogue have cast around yourselves? Or the fact that you are both Witches?" He smiled kindly at Nathan and me.

"Buh," I managed to say.

"Relax," Dr. Meyers suggested, walking farther into the main foyer from the back of the building, "there's no need to be upset. You've actually confirmed a working theory I've had for quite some time."

Nathan pushed his hands out with a small flourish. "Disperse," he said, and the protective circle winked out. He unlinked our feet, but remained beside me.

Dr. Meyer stood there, cool as a cucumber. "Might I suggest that we leave the building?"

The book slipped out of my fingers. It hit the floor with a bang and I cringed. "My nerves are shot to hell and gone," I said to Nathan as my knees began to wobble. "Get me out of here."

"Let's go," Nathan suggested.

The three of us exited the dormitory with Dr. Meyer leading the way. I followed behind and Nathan brought up the rear. We moved quickly, going out the way Nathan and I had come in. The door slammed shut behind us, on its own. I made it to the bottom of the steps, before my knees gave out. "Damn it," I muttered, grabbing onto the metal rail.

"Hey." Nathan grabbed me from behind. "*Hey.*" He

sounded concerned as he tucked his arm under my shoulders and helped me down the back steps.

"I should have had more than a soda for breakfast." I began to laugh. Why that seemed funny, I had not a clue.

"You're having a blood sugar crash," Nathan muttered. "You used a lot of magick and haven't had anything to eat all day." He took the camera from around my neck and handed it to Dr. Meyer. "That was pretty stupid, Ivy."

"Probably." I grinned at him. "Good thing *you're* smart then." I felt punch drunk, and couldn't help it as another laugh bubbled up.

Without another word, Nathan picked me up like a sack of potatoes and hauled me over to a nearby wooden bench. He dropped me down unceremoniously, so that I bounced when my butt hit the bench.

My head spun and my stomach lurched. For a couple of seconds I seriously considered throwing up. "Jeez, Pogue." I clutched my stomach, no longer laughing.

"Are you going to get sick?" he asked.

"No thanks to your caveman moves," I snarked.

Nathan took my messenger bag and began to root through it. "Do you have snacks in this monster sized bag of yours?"

I squinted at him, and also saw my brother walking towards us. "Bran?" I shook my head. "Why are you here?"

"I texted him before I entered the building," Dr.

Meyer explained, "told him to drive over. I had a feeling that I should." The older man shrugged.

"Ivy?" Bran called. "What's happened?"

I frowned at them all. I heard this loud buzzing sound in my ears, and my stomach roiled. "I am *not* going to pass out," I said— mostly to hear myself say it. It didn't seem to help. I gripped the bench and concentrated on my brother. I could see his lips moving and then... I found myself lying on the grass with my head in my Bran's lap.

"Weird," I muttered.

"Should we call an ambulance?" I heard Nathan ask.

"Don't you dare!" I said, offended.

"And, there you are." Bran smiled down at me.

"*Sonofabitch*," I said.

"I love you too, Ivy," Bran said dryly.

"Sorry," I said to Bran, and tried to sit up.

"I think that was directed at me," Nathan said cheerfully.

Bran helped me ease into a sitting position. *Oh gods! How embarrassing!* "I've never fainted before." I frowned at my brother. "Got knocked out, but never *passed* out... It sucks," I decided.

"What do you mean, you've been knocked out?" Nathan wanted to know.

"Long story," I said to Nathan.

"You didn't tell him about the abduction?" Bran said so only I could hear.

Nathan's eyebrows shot up to his hairline. I guess

he'd overheard. "Did you say, *abduction?*"

I looked significantly over at Dr. Meyer. "We can get into all of that later." I patted my chest and lap, realizing my camera was gone. "Where's my camera?"

"Right here, safe and sound." Dr. Meyer sat on the nearby bench in his khakis and green polo shirt, holding my camera.

"How are you feeling now?" Bran asked, helping me to stand.

"A little loopy, and I'm *starving*." I shivered and pulled my cardigan closer.

"Why don't we go get Ms. Bishop something to eat?" Dr. Meyer said. "Then we can all have a nice talk."

"Agreed," Bran said, taking my arm. "My car is right over here."

Nathan moved to my opposite side and took my other arm. "Let me help."

"For Goddess sake," I muttered, "I can walk on my own, unless this makes you two feel more manly."

"Shut up, Ivy," Bran and Nathan said simultaneously.

I sighed and let them take care of me. A short time later, I found myself sitting at a concrete table in the shade at a local fast food joint.

Nathan popped a soda in front of me and stuck in a straw. "Drink it."

"I know how to counteract a blood sugar crash, Pogue," I grumbled.

He swung a leg over the curved concrete bench and sat next to me. "Well then, you should have been smart enough not to put yourself in the position of ever suffering one."

I took a sip before I answered. "I've never done battle with, or tried to banish a book-throwing ghost before." I resisted the urge to make a face at him. "Cut me some slack, will ya?"

Bran and Dr. Meyer came out, each carrying a tray loaded with burgers and fries. Bran sat the tray down and handed me a wrapped double cheeseburger. "Eat," he said, sitting on my other side.

Dr. Meyer divvied up the fries. "Thank you Dr. Meyer," I said when he placed them in front of me.

"Please, call me Hal," he said.

I grinned at him. "Thanks, Hal." I dived in to my burger and fries, content to listen to Nathan and Hal discuss their parapsychology backgrounds. I finished my burger and felt better immediately.

Bran kicked my foot gently under the table. "The things you learn," he said, tilting his head at the two men.

"Aw check them out. They're so ghost-nerd cute," I said, nibbling on my remaining french fries.

Nathan swung his head around. "Did you really call me a ghost-nerd?" he said.

"I believe she said 'ghost-nerd cute'," Hal pointed out. "I'll take it as a compliment."

Nathan narrowed one eye at me, smiled and stole

some of my french fries in retaliation.

"Dr. Meyer," he said, "how did you get inside Crowly Hall?"

"The door was open." Dr. Meyer— Hal— waved a french fry at me. "How did you and Miss Bishop get in?"

"The door opened up for us, all by itself," Nathan said.

I shivered. "Almost as if the spirits wanted us to come in to witness the event."

Bran draped an arm over my shoulders. "So what happened in there?"

Nathan looked to me. "Do you want me to tell them?"

"Go ahead,' I said.

I was more than happy to let Nathan fill them in on what we'd experienced. It gave me the chance to let my system level. To Nathan's disappointment, the video recorded no clear images. It did, however, manage to record our voices and most of the ghosts'.

"Calamity?" Bran frowned at Nathan as he listened to the cell phone recording. "As in more to come? We've already had a serious accident at the archeological site, and a death on campus from the tornado."

"Well, things happen in threes," I said. "The archeologist getting injured was one, and the fatality from the storm at Crowly Hall would be two."

Hal adjusted his glasses. "Victoria Crowly's ghost

had in the past been considered a benign presence on campus," he said.

Nathan swiped a few more of my fries. "From what we've experienced she's becoming more aggressive."

"Desperate maybe," I said, thinking it over. "With the discovery of the remains, and the foundation of the house, the old surveyors maps and Mary Girard's journal... it's all coming to light. She was *nasty* when she went after us today, so I did my best to banish her from the Hall."

"Do you think it was successful?" Hal asked.

"Well, she left." I frowned as I thought about it. "She blew right through that spot on the wall where her portrait used to hang." I rubbed my forehead. "I don't know if she'll stay gone."

"When the information we discovered today gets out," Nathan said, "what happened to Prudence Thornton, and how they took her land. Victoria Crowly's reputation is going to be challenged."

Bran folded his arms over his chest. "The Board of Governors at the University will fight hard to protect the image of the school's founder."

"Exactly," Hal said, "they've built up quite the PR campaign over the years trying to showcase her as a brave pioneer and benevolent founder of the school."

"In the meantime," Nathan said, "we have to be on guard for another accident."

I closed my eyes and tried to recall what Prudence had said. *In the place where she sleeps... surrounded by an iron gate... bind her with blood...* I shuddered and glanced over at Nathan. "What do you think? Will the calamity be at the dig site, the dormitory, or someplace else?"

Nathan rubbed a hand over his chin. "Definitely someplace connected to Victoria or Prudence."

Bran wiped his hands on a napkin. "Most of the university is surrounded by decorative iron fencing. It's been in place for over a hundred years... That warning doesn't really narrow it down."

"The dig site is surrounded by fencing too," Nathan pointed out.

"We have to find a way to eliminate some of the possibilities..." I trailed off as an idea came to mind.

Bran narrowed his eyes at me. "I know that look."

Hal leaned closer across the table. "It would be almost impossible to foresee where and when the next incident would happen."

I winked at the older man. "It's not impossible, Hal. Especially when you have a Seer in the family."

CHAPTER TWELVE

As the waxing moon rose in the eastern sky my family, the Rousseaus and Dr. Meyer all gathered around the dining room table. Great Aunt Faye sat at the head with Bran on her right. Dr. Meyer, who appeared to be having the time of his life, was seated on her left. I wasn't sure if he was simply excited from being in the middle of a bunch of Witches, or if the manor's over-the-top Samhain décor had him put in a more bewitching mood.

Autumn sat at the foot of the table and Rene was to her left. Cypress and Marie sat between Dr. Meyer and Rene. I sat to Autumn's right with Nathan beside me. Bran had brought the old surveyor's maps to the manor. The maps of the campus were now spread out across the table. Autumn sat, quietly fidgeting with them.

"You okay?" I asked her. "Are you weirded out? Sitting at the family table, discussing all of the paranormal craziness with your boss at the museum?"

Autumn shrugged. "I gave up hoping for normal in

this town, years ago."

"Ivy," Cypress said, catching my attention from across the table, "I wish you would have called me today. You're my best friend. I should have been there." She held Merlin in her lap, and I had the uncomfortable experience of having two sets of amber colored eyes staring at me.

You hurt her feelings, I realized. "I'm sorry Cy," I said. "I wasn't trying to leave you out. It all just sort of happened."

Cypress gave my foot a light kick under the table. "I could have helped you. Did you ever think of that?"

I reached across the table for her hand and was about to apologize again, but when our hands clasped I got the strongest precognitive impression that I'd had in years. *Cypress was in danger.* I knew it like I knew my own name. And I had to make sure she stayed away from all of this ghost business... *Otherwise the next 'calamity' would involve her.* "You're my best friend," I said, struggling to keep my voice even. "You're as much my sister— as Holly is."

A 'sister', I realized with a sinking feeling. I felt my heart trip in my chest as my intuition revealed a truth to me. *Prudence had called Cypress and me sisters before — and what had she said today?* I held my breath and tried to recall it word for word. '*In the quiet place where she rests, surrounded by an iron gate; bind her with blood to protect another sister from her rage and hate.*' I gazed across the table at Cypress. There she sat;

my gorgeous, witchy BFF, and the sister of my heart, all rolled into one.

I'd lost one sister to magick gone wrong. I'd be damned if I'd lose another. I fought back tears and gave Cypress' fingers a light squeeze. "I'd do anything for you," I said. *Even lie to you, to keep you safe.*

Cypress held my hand for a moment longer, then let me go. "The next time you decide to face down ghosts," she said, "I want to be there."

I nodded, but said nothing. I slid my hand into my lap. I was surprised and relieved when, under the table, Nathan threaded his fingers through mine. *He knows. Nathan had figured out that my other 'sister' to protect was Cypress.* I glanced over at him.

Using the conversations all around us for cover, Nathan leaned closer to my ear. "I'll help you keep her safe," he murmured in my ear.

"Thank you," I said to him, as Lexie strolled into the room to join the family. I made a conscious effort to act as normal as possible. *Well, whatever normal was.*

Lexie pulled out the last empty chair next to Bran. "Finally," she said, and sat. "I got Morgan down for the night." She smiled politely at the historian across the table. "Hello Dr. Meyer."

"Please," he said, "call me Hal."

Marie, seated to the right of the man, grinned. "I have to say, you're taking all this remarkably well... Hal."

"I've known quite a few magickal practitioners in

my time," he said to Marie. "My wife was one."

"Was?" I asked.

"She passed away several years ago," Hal said quietly.

Aunt Faye put her hand over his. "I lost my husband ten years ago."

I watched my great-aunt and the doctor exchange glances. *What's this?* I thought. Aunt Faye was beautiful, but at least ten years older than the man. And if I was not mistaken... there was a little spark, a little *something* brewing between them.

Lexie leaned back in her chair, catching my eye behind Nathan's back. She wiggled her eyebrows. *So, Lexie sees it too,* I thought.

Nathan turned in his chair. "Dr. Meyer, what was your wife's family line— if you don't mind me asking?"

I tilted my head towards Nathan. "He's big on lineage."

"My wife's maiden name was Wardwell," Hal said.

Nathan thought that over. "There were several Wardwells imprisoned for witchcraft in Salem."

"Here we go," I groaned and sat back in my chair. "Autumn, do something quick before he launches into the 'my glorious ancestors are from Salem Village' speech."

"So are yours," Nathan said, sliding our joined hands to his lap.

I was so caught off guard by his move that I didn't

verbally retaliate. Which made me wonder: *Had he done it on purpose?*

"Dr. Meyer?" Autumn spoke up, pulling the surveyor's maps closer to her. "How long have you known about us?"

"I didn't know— not for sure. I speculated. That is until today." Hal glanced at Aunt Faye. "And I kept my theory to myself, I assure you."

"Besides witnessing Ivy's telekinesis, what tipped you off?" Autumn asked him.

"Hey! I was defending myself from a psychotic ghost," I said. "At least I didn't bean him with the book."

"Girlfriend," Cypress laughed, and scratched Merlin's kitty ears, "you've got to learn to keep things on the down-low."

Autumn rolled her eyes. "Subtlety, thy name is Ivy."

"Being subtle is vastly overrated," I said.

Hal chuckled. "Actually at first it was Autumn's uncanny knack for locating items at the museum archives that made me wonder. I began to notice that she had a horrible time with electronic equipment." He raised his eyebrows at Autumn. "I've seen lights blow out around you when you've stressed," he said.

On cue, right above us, the chandelier currently draped in fake spider webs and orange silk leaves for the holiday began to flicker.

"*Cher.*" Rene covered one of Autumn's hands with his. His touch seemed to have a calming effect on my cousin. She closed her eyes took in a deep breath, and blew it out. The flickering stopped.

I poked Autumn in the ribs, making her jump. "Who's *subtle* now, Witch?"

"Hey!" she laughed and jerked away.

"Girls," Aunt Faye warned, "behave yourselves. We have company."

Hal pulled an antique watch out of his pants pocket. "I actually started carrying this around. Autumn's personal energies have fried several digital watches of mine. This one seems to be safe." He held it out. "You have to wind it up, you see."

"So, Autumn is a SLIder," Nathan said, considering. "Makes sense."

"And *Autumn* is sitting right here," my cousin said, crossing her arms.

"Yes," Hal agreed with Nathan, "the phenomena of Street Lamp Interference... I've yet to see her blow up a street lamp though."

"Oh, she can," I said, grinning at the man. "I've seen her do it."

"Really?" Hal beamed right back at me.

I gently tugged my hand free of Nathan's. "You wanna see *slide*?" I asked, tapping on the maps with my fingernail. Taking Hal's hopeful expression for a go-ahead, I focused, and quickly turned my hands over, palms up. I raised my hands up a few inches and the surveyor's maps shot up, hovering in mid-air directly over our heads.

Hal jolted and began to laugh. "Wonderful," he said, watching the maps as they slid on top of each other.

Aunt Faye huffed out a breath, sending me a withering stare. "Ivy dear, simply because you *can* do something, doesn't mean you *should*."

I batted my eyelashes and tried to act innocent. "I only wanted the rest of the family to see what the maps looked like when they were overlaid and backlit."

Lexie whistled as she tipped her head up. "Wow. The orchard *was* right where the construction site is today."

Bran cleared his throat. "Okay Ivy, show's over. Now I think we should focus on the task at hand."

I sighed and let the maps go. They dropped down on their own. They gently fell to the floor, causing Aunt Faye to glare at me. "Even if you *can* do something..." I reminded her.

Cypress hopped up and retrieved the maps. Merlin scampered away, and my friend set the large pages back on the table. I could see she was biting her lip to keep from laughing.

Autumn spread her hands over the maps again. "So you want me to dowse and see if I can find the location for the next paranormal event?"

"Do you want me to help?" I asked her. "I could lend energy."

Autumn pulled a crystal pendulum out of her pocket. "Sure, I bet your energy would help, since you've been at the center of this."

I stood up and walked around the table to stand

behind Autumn's chair. Cypress sat quietly, and appeared very unhappy. "Cypress," I said, holding out my hand to her, "I think you should help with this." I silently prayed that I was doing the right thing. *How was I supposed to keep her safe, and not hurt her feelings in the process?*

Cypress' smile lit up the dining room. "I'd be happy to." She rose to her feet and ranged herself on the opposite side of Autumn. "We're in this together, after all," she said.

***

By the time we had finished, we'd identified three potential "hot spots". Cypress and I had each gently rested a hand on one of Autumn's shoulders. Autumn took a deep breath and stretched her right arm out over the map, the pendulum dangling from her fingers on its silken cord. She waited until the pendulum was at rest, and then began to sweep her hand slowly over the map.

The pendulum reacted the most strongly at three locations. The problem was, we'd already had encounters at each of the locations before. The first had been Crowly Hall. The second had been the archeological dig/ Prudence's cabin/ future construction site, and the third was at the campus cemeteries.

The last location had made my heart jump to my throat.

There. I realized. *It would be at the little cemeteries*

that I would have to face down Victoria Crowly's ghost — and hopefully for the last time.

It was late by the time Dr. Meyer and the Rousseaus had left. Now, a single lamp burned low in the family room. The flickering light from the fire and the decorated mantle lit up the room in a warm orange glow.

After Autumn had said goodnight, and Bran and Lexie had gone up to bed, Nathan seemed in no hurry to leave. Nathan slouched on one end of the couch, and I curled up at the other end, opposite of him, as we sat discussing the day's events. Aunt Faye had finally retired for the night, and Nathan and I were alone.

I confided quietly to Nathan that I'd figured out what Prudence had meant today. *In the quiet place where she rests,* had to mean her grave. It was surrounded by an iron fence. Then the *'bind her with blood'*— was using magick to accomplish it obviously. All to *'protect another sister from her rage and hate.'* That other sister I had to protect, being Cypress.

Frustrated and afraid for my friend, I got up and added another log to the fire in the fireplace. I stood at the hearth listening to the snap and crackle of the fire, and watched the flames lick at the logs. "So what do you think?" I asked him.

"I think you are right about the cemetery being the correct location," Nathan said. "Plus with the veil between the worlds being at its thinnest now, we have a better magickal chance of success for the binding."

I crossed my arms. "I wonder what is different this year that it's making it easier for so many ghosts to come through?"

"When Prudence's remains were disturbed and we excavated finding the foundation of her home, it opened up everything. The accidental discovery of human remains, and or dramatic changes to the landscape, often kicks off a haunting."

I nodded. "When they first clear cut the old orchard, to begin construction of the new museum, that's when I discerned the sour energy on campus. Everything else flowed out and picked up speed after that."

"I think we can set things right," Nathan said. "I'm starting to believe that you and I were *meant* to be the ones to do this."

"A couple of Witches from very different backgrounds and traditions taking on campus ghosts... What could possibly go wrong?" I groused.

"It's those differences that are going to make us successful."

I blew out a breath. "So much for a quiet Samhain."

"You know, I've never seen a house decorated for Samhain like this before," Nathan said.

Thrown by the change of topic, and ready for an argument, I arched a brow at him, "Is that a snide comment, Pogue?"

"No." He sat up and focused on me. "It's amazing. Especially the big black decorated tree in the foyer. Makes me think of one of those magazine photo shoots for Halloween."

I considered the mantle over the fireplace. This year a trio of black metal lanterns, holding flickering LED pillars, rested on the left end of the mantle. A clever stack of old books was centered, and a decorated velvet Witch's hat rested on top of them. A porcelain figure of a black cat was beside the books, and at the opposite side of the thick mantle, a large Cinderella type pumpkin was displayed resting on top of an urn. Clusters of raffia peeked out from under the big fat pumpkin, while an assortment of other orange pumpkins were arranged around the base of the urn.

"It's my favorite time of year," I said, running my fingers across the lush, silk garland of orange, red, and brown oak leaves that draped across the edge of the mantle. Autumn had worked tiny orange fairy lights into the garland, and they twinkled ever so slightly. My mother's old willow broom rested along the side of the fireplace, and I had tied the big orange and black ribbon on the handle myself.

"I bet every kid in the neighborhood comes here on Halloween for trick-or-treating," Nathan said.

"This is nothing," I warned him. "Wait until you see what goes in the front yard in a few weeks. A dozen carved jack-o'-lanterns, a bunch of cool props, and we even use a fog machine."

"It sounds great," Nathan said.

I thought I heard a little wistfulness in his voice. "Do you have any plans for the thirty-first?" I asked.

Nathan stood up and walked over to me. "No, I don't."

"You are welcome to drop by over here. We can always use another body," I said, casually.

Nathan laughed at the double entendre. He stepped closer— closer than he ever had before. "Today was intense," he said, staring down into my eyes.

"It really was." I had to tip my head back to maintain eye contact. "I'm truly scared for Cypress," I admitted quietly.

"I meant what I said, earlier," he said. "I'll help you keep her safe."

Nothing he could have said would have meant more to me. "Thank you." I moistened my lips against a mouth that had suddenly gone dry. I froze, wondering how that might have been interpreted.

Nathan leaned over, his mouth a breath from mine. I held my breath and waited.

I'm not sure who moved first. Maybe I jumped up in his arms, or maybe he scooped me up off the floor. But the next thing I knew for sure— his mouth was on mine, my arms were tight around his neck while his hands were all over me. I opened my mouth to his as he slid his hands down over my backside. I wrapped my legs around his waist and held on. I felt him move a few steps and we dropped down to the nearby couch.

Before I knew it my sweater was gone. The t-shirt followed soon after. I reached out for his gray shirt and pulled it free from his waistband. We tugged it off together and when he latched his mouth back on mine I let out an appreciative purr at the feelings of our chests being pressed together. I pulled back and ran my mouth down his gorgeous chest.

"Mmmm," I murmured, cruising my mouth over some very fine pectorals and defined abs. His hands clenched in my hair, and before I could enjoy myself too much he pulled me back up to his mouth.

I felt him grope for my bra closure, and after a few moments he gave up, turning me in his arms to unfasten the black lace bra. Once freed, he reached around from behind and filled his hands with my breasts. I found myself braced against the arm of the couch while he helped himself. He kissed his way down my back and up my shoulders. I felt him unzip my jeans and his hand slid down.

I grabbed his hand. "Nathan," I managed.

He flexed his fingers, and I damn near came right there and then.

I tossed my head back to look at him. "We have to stop. I don't have any protection." I made myself say it.

The expression on his face had every one of my muscles clenching. He slid his hand free, spun me in his arms, and I landed on my back under him on the sofa. He kissed my breasts, his teeth teasing and tormenting. "You smell like roses," he said.

"Nathan," I said, reaching out for him. My fingers landed on the proof of his desire. Every coherent thought in my head vanished.

His hand covered mine, and we both froze. I stared into his eyes and he into mine. "We have to stop..." he gritted out.

"We have to," I gasped, easing my hand away.

"I know," he said, leaning into my throat. His stubble rasped against my skin. For a few moments we simply held each other, panting.

Nathan slowly eased back to the other end of the couch. He stared at me for a long moment, and I let him. No point in acting shy now. He'd already had his hands and mouth all over my upper body. And Goddess knows I was enjoying the view of him shirtless myself.

"Holy crap." I blew out a breath and stared at the ceiling. Eventually I sat up, and reached for my bra. I hooked it in the front and spun it around to the back. I looped my arms through the straps, stood up and scooped the girls into the lace bra cups.

I picked up my t-shirt and felt more than heard him stand behind me. "I like this," he said as his lips rubbed over the crescent moon and star tattoo on my right shoulder.

"Thanks, it's the family's magickal crest," I said.

He pulled back and pressed a kiss to the top of my head. For a moment I stood there with my head resting against his chest. "Ivy," he said, and took a steadying breath.

We stepped apart. I pulled my t-shirt back on and watched him scoop up his own shirt from the floor. "I'd say something like, I'm not sure what just happened here." I cleared my throat. "But that seems stupid."

Nathan's blue-gray eyes were almost lit up as he stood still, holding his shirt. "We're attracted to each other and we acted on it."

"Yeah, but I don't usually do this..." I trailed off, trying to figure the best way to say it. "I have never done the 'we almost had sex' thing in my house. With my family right upstairs, with someone I don't know very well." I blew out a breath. "I don't even know if you are in a relationship with someone else."

"I'm not," he said.

"Well that's something, anyway," I said. He continued to stand there— in no rush to leave. "Do me a favor Pogue," I said, "put your shirt back on."

He grinned at that. "Maybe I was wanting to show you *my* tattoo."

Pleased that he was trying to lighten the mood I arched an eyebrow at him. "Oh yeah? Where's it at?" I gave him the once over, but saw no ink on the front of his body.

He shrugged his shirt on. "You'll have to guess."

"I bet it's on your butt."

He blinked, clearly offended. "No."

I tapped my finger against my lips as I considered. "Yeah, I think it's a skull and crossbones. Something bad-ass and butch."

"Please." He rolled his eyes.

"Tramp stamp?" I said. "A butterfly, maybe?"

He laughed, and bent down and gave me a quick

kiss. "Nope."

I smiled up at him, reached around and gave his back side a friendly pat. "I'm betting it's there."

"Maybe I'll show you sometime," Nathan said.

"Maybe I'll let you." I kissed him back.

Nathan ended the kiss. He took a deep breath and blew it out slowly. "I should go," he said, resting his forehead against mine.

I went and got his denim jacket for him and, playing the good hostess, I walked him out onto the front porch. The orange Halloween lights lit up the front porch with a festive glow. He went down a few steps, stopped and grinned at the creepy scarecrow that loomed over the front gardens. He walked back to me. For once we were eye to eye.

"Good night, Nathan," I said.

"Ivy." He leaned in and kissed me lightly. "I'll call you in the morning?"

"Sure." I smiled. "But not too early."

Nathan laughed and moved quickly down the steps. I watched as he went down the front sidewalk and out the gate. I went back to the front door and waited until I heard his car start up, I saw him wave, and I let myself back in the door, locking it behind me.

I clicked off the lamp in the family room, closed the glass doors on the fireplace, and headed for the foyer. The decorated Halloween tree illuminated the main entrance of the manor and the staircase nicely. I trailed my fingers along the black branches of the artificial tree and swung around to head up the stairs— almost walking straight through my grandmother's ghost.

I stifled a scream. "Jeez!" I jumped back. "Grandma Rose, you scared the crap outta me!"

My grandmother's ghost stood on the bottom step, resting her elbow on the banister. As she had the first two times I'd seen her appear in the manor, she wore her bright pink sweater and jeans. Her silly straw gardening hat hung down her back. "Well." She narrowed her eyes at me.

I pressed a hand to my heart. "Well, what?"

"You're having yourself quite the adventure, aren't you?"

I blushed. *Oh my Goddess, how long had my grandmother's ghost been hanging around? How much had she seen?* "Have you been spying on me?"

She folded her arms. "I think 'keeping an eye on you' is the better way to say it."

I shook my head. "That's downright creepy."

"You're blushing," she said.

"I am *not*," I hissed. "Thinning veil or not, I am *really* tired of ghosts right now." I stepped around her and marched up the stairs with her gentle laughter following me.

I made it into my room and quietly closed the bedroom door. I hit the lights, but only Merlin was there. His highness was sprawled, belly up, in the middle of my bed. Quickly I stripped out of my clothes and dropped them on the floor. I grabbed my night shirt from the hook behind the bathroom door and pulled it over my head.

Exhausted, I pulled back the covers and jumped in the big bed. Merlin muttered and rolled over. I shut my eyes and willed myself to sleep.

I was starting to drift off when I heard, "Sleep well, sweetheart."

"G'night Grandma," I mumbled. I smiled when I felt a kiss pressed to the top of my head.

CHAPTER THIRTEEN

Dreams chased me all night long. Disjointed images from the past, the present, and the probable future—one after another they melded and ran together.
Me calling desperately to Nathan, our hands clasped together... Victoria Crowly's distorted face, shrieking and wailing... The earth shaking, tree branches snapping in storm winds... The surveyor's maps, backlit, and the location of the old orchard illuminated... Cypress and I huddling in the cellar of the dormitory while the tornado roared overhead...Wrapping Nathan's wrist with the piece of ivy vine... The foreman uncovering the skull at the construction site... Making love with Nathan in front of the fireplace... Jessica sleepwalking in Crowly Hall...Prudence Thornton sobbing about her stolen land... Cypress flipping the couch out of the way by her fingertips to get to Jessica... Nathan casting a circle around Victoria Crowly's tombstone, candles blowing out, blood dripping from my fist, and falling down on

the green grass... Cypress running towards me, while lightning struck far too close... A roll cloud that swallowed the world...

I sat up covered in sweat, my chest heaving. The sun was up, barely. I could tell it was early from the position of the light creeping in the windows. My phone was ringing, and it took me a minute before I could figure out what to do about that. I dropped my head in my hands and ignored the phone, as the dreams replayed in my mind.

Merlin walked over and sat in my lap. I grunted and patted his head.

When the phone started to ring again, I swore and felt around on the night stand. I found my phone and hit the accept button on the screen. "*What?*" I snarled into the phone.

"Ivy?" Nathan's voice sounded through the phone. "Sorry, did I wake you up?"

I flung myself back on the pillows and tossed an arm over my eyes. "Nathan you should know, before we go any further... I am *not* a morning person."

He chuckled. "Are you alright?" he asked.

It took me a second to answer. "Rough night," I said. "Bad dreams. Give me a second."

"Okay."

Merlin walked up my chest and batted at my nose. "Merlin!" I pulled my face away. In retaliation the cat stuck his paw right in my mouth. "Aack!" I rolled over, dislodging the cat.

"What's going on?" Nathan said, while Merlin howled.

"Nathan, can you hang on for a couple of minutes?" I asked, wiping cat hair off my mouth with the back of my hand.

"Sure," he said.

I dropped the phone on my pillow, rolled out of bed and staggered to the bathroom. I splashed some cold water on my face, brushed my teeth, and used mouthwash for good measure. All while Merlin sat on the sink and silently supervised. "You are a rotten cat," I told him, patting my face dry with a towel.

Merlin merely flipped his tail in answer.

I squinted at the sunlight as I climbed back into bed. I cleared my throat and picked up the phone. "Go ahead caller, you're on the air," I said, pulling the covers up to my chin.

Nathan laughed. "You sound awake now."

"Whether I like it or not," I said, yawning. "What's up?"

"You said earlier that you'd had bad dreams last night?" He paused, then asked, "Precognitive dreams?"

"It was a weird mixture. Past, present, and the future." I shuddered recalling the blood on the grass. "I dreamed of us doing a binding ritual at the campus cemetery. It was spooky."

"Was Cypress in the dreams?" Nathan's voice was soft, but serious.

"She showed up off and on in my dreams," I said.

"Why?"

"Because Cypress was in *my* dreams too. She was running towards me, and shouting."

I flashed back to my dream images. "That's similar to what I dreamt. And to be honest, it scares me that she was there in those dreams. I want her far away from all of this." I swallowed past the emotions that welled up. "Was there a storm in your dream?"

"Yeah," Nathan sighed. "Thunder, lightning, and this huge rumbling cloud—"

"A roll cloud?" I said, pushing the covers aside.

"What's a roll cloud?" Nathan asked.

"Think of a massive storm front that looks like a waterfall of clouds. If you want to get technical they are called arcus clouds— you live in the Midwest long enough, east coast boy, and you'll see one."

"Do they usually precede a tornado?" Nathan asked.

"Or a severe thunderstorm."

"Was there a roll cloud before the tornado last month?"

"No, not that I remember." I waited for him to comment, but he remained silent. "So, what are you thinking?" I finally asked, when I could stand the silence no more.

"I think it's significant that we both had similar dreams about a storm and Cypress."

"I do too." I sighed. "I think the binding we need to do is to *protect* Cypress, specifically."

"How do you feel about breakfast?" Nathan asked.

"I have very fond feelings for breakfast. And for waking me up this early in the morning, you are definitely buying me something that involves both sugar and caffeine."

A half hour later Nathan and I were crammed into a little café table next to the front window of the Blue Moon Bakery. As usual the place was hopping, but since it was a Sunday morning, the bakery was doubly busy. People waited in line in front of the deep glass display cases for doughnuts, pastries, and muffins.

A couple of Hipster students snagged the last of the tables across from us. "I love your Halloween sweatshirt," the girl said to me.

I glanced down. I smiled in response to her well intended compliment— but didn't have the heart to tell her that for me, this was hardly seasonal wear. My gray sweatshirt had a large vintage-style illustration of a skull printed on the front of it. I'd layered that over a white blouse that featured silver studs on the collar and folded back cuffs.

Nathan sipped his coffee and glanced around the bakery. "Popular place," he said, taking in the pale blue walls and the cheeky vintage advertising signs for cakes, fresh milk and butter.

I took a bite of my cake doughnut, and the crumbly cinnamon topping melted in my mouth. Crumbs rolled down my shirt and landed in the lap of my blue jeans.

"You have powdered sugar on your chin." Nathan grinned.

I brushed the crumbs off my shirt. "A small price to pay," I said, with my mouth full. "This is my favorite kind."

Nathan sat his blueberry muffin down and reached out with a paper napkin. "I can see that." He brushed the powdered sugar away from my mouth.

I broke off a piece of doughnut and handed it over. "Here, try it."

"It's good," Nathan said a moment later. "Really good."

"Mr. Jacobs has the magick touch when it comes to doughnuts." Nathan's mouth was now covered in powdered sugar and cinnamon crumbles too. "Come here." I crooked a finger at him, grabbed a paper napkin and returned the favor.

Nathan reached up for my hand, and our eyes met and held. I suppressed a little shiver, remembering how close we'd come to having sex last night. I guess he was thinking the same thing, because the teasing light went out of his eyes. Nathan shifted forward in his chair. I leaned closer across the little table towards him. Our lips were about to meet when—

"If it isn't my favorite little shutterbug." The spell broken, Nathan and I sat back. I glanced up to see Mr. Jacobs grab the one empty chair left and pull it up to our little table.

"Hi ya, Oliver." I smiled in resignation as he joined us.

Oliver Jacobs, baker extraordinaire, sat at our table,

all good will and cheer. He was my height, stocky and dressed in his typical work uniform with a blue apron and white ball cap. The older man was one of my favorite people, not simply because he made amazing pastries; but because he was down-to-earth, a loving father and grandpa, had a great sense of humor, and was one hell of a powerful Witch.

"Who's your friend?" Oliver asked me, his blue eyes twinkling with mischief.

I introduced him to Nathan and watched as they shook hands. I didn't bother to warn Nathan that Oliver would use the opportunity to scan him. I lifted my soda and took a sip, wondering how Nathan would handle it all.

Nathan's eyes narrowed before he let go of the baker's hand. "Nice to meet you, Mr. Jacobs." He nodded politely.

Oliver grinned at Nathan. "Call me Oliver." He rested his elbows on the little table and leaned in closer to the two of us. "I hear you've both been real busy over on campus."

I laughed. "That's one way to put it."

"How did you know—" Nathan began.

"He's on the local high council," I explained, and knowing Nathan I added, "Oliver is also the head of the Jacobs' family line."

Oliver leaned conspiratorially close. "Faye called me last night, brought me up to speed on the newest paranormal developments. I want you both to be careful, you hear me?"

"No worries," I said, going for a casual vibe. *It wasn't like I could discuss everything in a crowded bakery.* I thought, picking up my second crumb doughnut.

Oliver reached out and touched the sleeve of Nathan's denim jacket. He rested his other hand over mine, and I froze. All the background noise of the bakery faded away. It was as if the three of us sat in our own little triangular shaped bubble.

"Impressive," Nathan breathed, studying the baker and the spell he'd woven around the three of us with appreciation.

The power I felt from the man didn't frighten me. I'd known Oliver Jacobs my whole life— I trusted him, and more, I *respected* him. If he was doing magick in public, it was for a damn good reason. "The dreams you two share," Oliver said, "don't dismiss them, you received the foretelling for a reason."

I wasn't surprised that Oliver knew that, as talented of a practitioner as he was, so I nodded in agreement. "I dreamed of working a ritual to bind Victoria Crowly's spirit to her grave," I said softly. "In my dreams I saw drops of blood running down my fingers, and burning candles at her gravesite."

"That's an intense type of magick," Oliver warned us.

"I know it's hard-core." I blew out my cheeks. "But I think that's what it will take to stop any more accidents from happening at the dig site, at Crowly Hall, and most importantly to protect Cypress."

"We'll have to be very careful doing the binding," Nathan agreed. "We'd be walking the edge of the darker magicks."

"I don't think we have much of a choice," I said. "It's all coming to a head, and soon."

"Tonight." Oliver nodded in confirmation. "Are you both ready?"

My gut clenched of what needed to be done in comparison to my puny spell casting ability. I dropped my eyes down to my lap. "Of course I'll do the best I can, but without Holly..."

"Ivy." Nathan tipped my chin up with a gentle finger. "The only thing that is holding back your success with solo magick is a lack of faith in your own abilities."

"Remember, the Principle of Mentalism states: *Thought creates*," Oliver said. "You have unlimited potential, young lady. Master your mind, and you can accomplish anything."

He was right. They both were. "Mind over matter," I said to them. "The down and dirty definition of magick."

"Exactly." Nathan gave my cheek a caress and sat back.

The emotion that welled up had me fighting to keep my voice steady. "I'd do *anything* to protect the people I love," I said, "and I will keep Cypress safe. No matter what it takes."

Oliver sat back and clapped his hands together. With a *pop* the noise of the busy bakery rushed back in. "Well, there you go," he said in a conversational tone of voice, obviously pleased at the outcome of our chat. Oliver stood and slid the chair back to its table. He turned back to Nathan and stuck out his hand. "Pleasure meeting you."

"Likewise." Nathan smiled and seemed to mean it as he clasped hands with the baker.

"Good luck tonight," Oliver said to the both of us.

I jumped to my feet and hugged the older man. He might have been my height, but he was strong. Oliver gave me a big bear hug that lifted me off my feet, and had me giggling. "Thanks for the pep talk," I said.

"Any time." Oliver tipped his ball cap and went back to work.

I sat back at the little café table with Nathan. "So, tonight is when it's all going to go down."

"We have all day," Nathan said. "I have a few things — tools and supplies back at my apartment that would help."

"If we could stop at the manor first, I have a few things I'd like to add to that supply list."

"Sure," Nathan agreed. "We could put everything together at my place, it's practically on campus, and come up with a game plan."

I nodded mentally going over a list of supplies I would want to bring along. Binding a ghost to her grave was going to take effort and planning. I took a big bite of my doughnut and ignored the falling crumbs. I had a feeling I was going to need the carbs.

***

Nathan's place was actually in an old three story home that had been converted into several grad student apartments. The old building was right across the street from Hyde Theater, which also meant it was easy walking distance from the campus cemeteries. I hauled my hooded jacket and messenger bag up three flights of stairs to the top floor. Nathan had my backpack slung over one shoulder as he stopped to unlock his front door.

Nathan, it turned out, was a tidy soul. The apartment wasn't large— a combined living/ kitchen area and one small bedroom. I poked my head in his bedroom and saw a nice computer desk and bookshelf set up on the facing wall. A queen size bed was shoved against the left wall, and a beat up nightstand held a small lamp. To the right side of the bedroom was the bath, and beyond that a closed door that I assumed led to a closet.

Hardwood floors, still in excellent shape, ran throughout the apartment. I walked across a charcoal area rug, and over to his well-used blue sofa and sat down. Nathan dumped my backpack beside a large trunk that served for a coffee table. We spent the next several hours drafting out a magickal game plan. Ritual elements were suggested, discarded, or accepted and then tweaked to compliment our current situation.

I sat shoulder to shoulder with Nathan as we drafted the banishing ritual on his laptop. We decided to keep the ritual brief, as it minimized our chances of being interrupted or worse— busted by campus security. We tried to take into consideration our location, the lack of privacy at the campus cemeteries, the time of sunset, the phase of the moon, and even the weather. I was unsurprised to see that a chance for severe thunderstorms had been added to the local forecast.

After we settled on the mechanics of the spell, we took a hard look at the tools we'd each chosen to use, and at Nathan's suggestion we cast a circle together in his apartment. We sat cross legged and facing each other on the carpet, inside the ritual circle. Surrounded by white candles and the fragrant smoke of dragon's blood incense, we worked together to align our personal energies. We were deliberately careful to take the time to ground and prepare for the work ahead of us; and lastly to sterilize my athame and also to empower all of our other magickal tools for protection, and success.

By the time we had finished, it was late afternoon. As predicted, the weather had begun to change. I stood at his windows, watching a roll cloud precede the storm front. I wasn't sure if that was comforting that another element of the dream was in play, or if that made me more determined to get this over with. Nathan ordered hearty sub sandwiches and we dug in, since food, especially protein and carbs, were another source of magickal fuel. It was a very practical sort of magick. By the time the sun had set it was full dark, and we were packed, prepared, and ready to go.

Campus was typically quiet on Sunday evenings, and that combined with the surrounding trees, the coming rain, and low traffic area around the cemeteries, I figured we had a good shot of going about our business unnoticed. However, the first thing Nathan and I did once we arrived was to cast a reluctance over the immediate area. I set my supplies out quickly, and no sooner had Nathan finished lighting the last of the quarter candles when rain began to lightly fall. I stood outside the gate of the plot where Victoria Crowly and her sister Melinda rested and pulled my hood up on my black, pleather jacket and tugged the zipper higher.

Nathan buttoned the top of his black oilskin coat, which I thought made him look like a soldier from colonial times... or maybe a pirate... With effort, I pulled my wandering mind back to attention and focused on the task at hand.

A low roll of distant thunder had me frowning up at the sky. We'd need those candles to continue to burn, no matter what. On impulse, I knelt down next to the candle in the northern quarter and held my hand out. "If these flames are extinguished in the physical, they will shine on in the astral realm until we open the circle. As I will it, so must it be."

"So mote it be." Nathan formally echoed my words. He held out a hand to me, I took it and rose to my feet.

We stepped inside of the little graveyard, and I waited, silent and respectful, for him to cast the ritual circle. To cover our bets, Nathan performed The Lesser Banishing Ritual of the Pentagram. As he intoned the Hebrew words at each quarter, I moved with him. When we finished I *felt*, more than I saw, the energy roll into place. I visualized, in my mind's eye, energy running out and meeting the ring of ritual candles that were nestled in the grass a few feet beyond the fence of the family plot.

"Ready?" Nathan asked. At my nod, he moved to the opposite side of the row of headstones and stood next to Melinda's crypt.

As agreed, I continued with the ritual. "Earth, air, fire and water, circle 'round and about; protect us well and keep passerbys out." I moved to the center of the circle and held my hands up to the sky. "In this time and in this hour, we ask the Lord and Lady to lend us their power..." When I finished the invocation, I nodded to him.

Moving back to the opposite side of the circle across from Nathan, I picked up a carton of salt. *Mind over matter. Thought creates. I can do this.* The words ran though my head as I poured some into my hand and began the binding. I sprinkled salt on top of the grass that grew over the grave. "By the power of earth, and with salt; Victoria Crowly, I bind you to your grave," I said.

The wind started to pick up, and the tree branches

began to creak and sway in the storm winds. I pulled my athame from the sheath at my waist. The short double-sided blade had never cut anything physically before. The fact that I was about to use it now for that very purpose meant that it would be useless to me in the future. However, a willing sacrifice would give our binding magick a boost like nothing else. I was prepared to release, or sacrifice, one of my favorite tools. And I was *willing* to suffer a little pain to add a few drops of my own blood to the binding ritual.

I used the tip of the knife and drew a small shallow cut beneath my thumb in the meatiest part of the palm of my hand. I hissed at the burn, and I tucked the athame back in its sheath. I squeezed my left hand into a fist and kept applying pressure, waiting for the blood to well up. In a few moments I could feel blood begin to pool in my hand.

I held my hand out over the grave. "By blood I bind you to your grave Victoria Crowly." The first of the drops spilled free, and I watched as they seemed to fall almost in slow motion from my fist and towards the grass. I took a deep breath and prepared myself for the third and final part of the ritual. "By my will I—"

I gasped and almost fell on my butt when Victoria Crowly materialized directly behind her tombstone. Even semi transparent, it was obvious that she was not happy to see me.

"Witch!" she snarled, as the rain picked up. The wind seemed to howl over us, and one by one the quarter candles went out. "I burned one of your kind out of her home. I'll do worse to you if you don't stop this evil!"

"Keep going," Nathan called over the wind. "Ivy keep going!"

I faced her down. "You nasty old hag," I said. "Your sister would be ashamed of you for what you've done!"

"Ivy!" Cypress was suddenly beside me, appearing out of nowhere.

"Cy, what the hell are you doing here?" I said, shoving her behind me to keep her farther away from Victoria. We shuffled around and knocked over the salt. It poured out onto the grass. "Stop!" I squeezed her arm to get her attention. "What'd you do? Jump through the reluctance's boundary, *and* the ritual circle?"

Cypress scowled at me. "You bet your ass I did." Soaking wet, her curls sprang around her face. "I *knew* you'd try something stupid."

"It's not safe for you here...," I tried to tell her, noticing that Victoria's ghost seemed to grow larger as we bickered.

Cypress faced the ghost. "You lured Jessica out of her room, and caused the accident with the archeologist at the dig site!"

"You are beneath me, I do not answer to your kind." Victoria sneered at Cypress.

"You bigoted old bitch!" Cypress gasped.

Victoria's ghost seemed to smile. "That Thornton woman should have *stayed* buried," she muttered.

Cypress reached down and chucked a handful of salt over the tombstone and at the spirit. Infuriated, Cypress hissed out something in French, and the ghost shrank back.

"Cypress!" Nathan called. "Don't feed into her anger, it only gives the spirit more power."

"Cypress, Cy!" I pleaded, yanking her back before she dove after the ghost. "I've got this. Trust me." I tugged Cypress away by her blue raincoat. "Go. Help Nathan hold the boundaries of the circle."

Cypress moved back a few steps, arranging herself centrally between Nathan and I. "Nathan?" she called over the storm. "Get ready!" I had a second to brace myself, and then she tossed her hands down. Thunder cracked, and a triangle of energy burned bright and white within the once barely visible circle.

I felt the infusion of power that Cypress added to the area. The three of us stood at the points of that energetic triangle, facing down the ghost— who suddenly seemed very corporeal— even as the storm intensified.

"You're facing the three of us now," I said to the ghost. I took a deep breath and started over again. "By the power of earth and with salt; I bind you forever to your grave, Victoria Crowly."

"I bind you from causing harm, Victoria Crowly," Cypress begin to spontaneously chant over and over, even as the storm raged.

"No!" Victoria shrieked. "No! You've barred me from my home, you won't trap me here."

I took out my athame and prepared to make another cut to my palm. The rain had washed my blood away from before. And I needed both blood *and* my will to finish the spell. "By the power of blood—" My words ended as I took an unexpected blow to the face. The force of the strike made my head snap to the side, and had my ears ringing.

"I will crush you!" Victoria raged.

"Ivy!" Cypress yelled.

"Bitch," I said, as a copper taste filled my mouth. I shook my head to clear it, and spit out blood.

"Ivy, finish the ritual!" Nathan called.

I straightened and focused on the ghost. *Mind over matter.* I reminded myself. *I would do this thing.* I wiped the blood away with the palm of my hand, and then I swiped the flat of the athame's blade over my hand and raised it high.

"By my blood I bind you from ever causing harm again, Victoria Crowly." I flung the athame down, along with my power, and it stuck deep, vibrating into the ground directly in front of the tombstone. "By my *will* I bind you forever to your grave," I said, and felt the spell come together and sink into the soil around me. "By salt, blood and will, you are bound. No escape will ever be found."

If a ghost could appear horrified, this one did. "You can't!" she said.

"I *have*." I reached out for Cypress' hand. "By the power of three times three; forever bound Victoria

Crowly, you shall be."

"Forever bound Victoria Crowly, you shall be," Cypress said.

Nathan stepped in and took Cy's other hand. "Forever bound Victoria Crowly, you shall be." At the third repetition, the ghost seemed to dissolve.

I heard the crack and, without looking, I *knew* what was happening. I shoved Cypress hard to the right, tackling her to the ground. A horrible rushing sound came from above and behind us as a tree started to fall. Nathan dove on top of Cypress and I, and the tree went down— just to the left of us. With a deafening *boom*, the ground shook. An energetic ripple rolled out and then dissipated.

For a few seconds the three of us stayed down. "Nathan?" I asked. "Cy, are you okay?"

"I am," Nathan said, starting to shift. "How about you?"

"I'm okay." I sat up slowly.

"You guys are squashing me!" Cypress complained, shoving free.

"Sorry," Nathan said, and the three of us stayed where we were, sitting in the rain, and staring in amazement. The crown of the tree was several yards away, but one side of the metal fencing was smashed. The massive trunk had come down *very* close to us.

I gulped. "Oh my Goddess." The trunk of the tree was less than six feet away, and right along the outside of the triangle of power Cypress had thrown down. That triangle pulsed once and began to fade.

"Wow," Cypress said.

"It's over," I said, lifting my face to the rain. "Can you feel it? The whole atmosphere is different." Relieved, I started to smile.

Nathan stood and pulled Cypress and me up. "I'll say this, you William's Ford Witches know how to show a guy a good time."

I snorted out a laugh and took a half hearted swipe at him. "Jeez, Pogue."

"Come here," he said, tugging me to him. I stood on my tiptoes and met him half way for his kiss.

"Umm hmm, I thought so," Cypress said as the kiss continued. "You two squabbled way too much for there *not* to be some chemistry brewing."

I pulled slightly away from Nathan and grinned at Cypress. "Come here, you." I grabbed the sleeve of her raincoat, and pulled her close. After a moment, I held out an arm to Nathan.

"Wow, ultimate guy fantasy," Nathan joked, and joined the group hug.

I reached up and yanked on his hair in retaliation for the comment. "Dream on, Pogue," I said, laughing.

For a moment the three of us stood holding each other, then something else caught my eye. "Look at that," I said, pointing to the pink granite marker.

Nathan turned for a closer inspection. "The top corner of Victoria Crowly's headstone has been broken off."

I sniffed. "It's what she gets for trying to crush me and my BFF."

"Karmic justice," Cypress said, firmly. "She deserved it."

Before I could respond to Cypress, a new spirit shimmered to life in front of us. I gawked at the image of a pretty young woman who hummed a lullaby to a baby in her arms.

I knew who this was. "You're Melinda, aren't you?" I said.

She nodded. "I am. Thank you for helping her. She's been lost for so long."

"Are you talking about Victoria or Prudence?" Cypress asked her.

"Both." The spirit moved to the right and hovered over the one stone crypt in the cemetery. "Now my sister *and* my friend can be at peace." She nodded once and seemed to fade back into the top of the crypt.

The three of us stood for a few moments, waiting and watching. But all remained quiet and the rain was slowing.

"We should go," Nathan said finally. "Someone will notice the tree and the damage to the family plot."

"Okay," I said. "Maybe we can go back to your place and clean up and dry out a bit," I suggested.

"Give me a second, here," Nathan said. He quickly released the elements, thanked the gods, and opened the circle, letting the reluctance magick disperse.

Cypress knelt down and grounded her triangle of

power into the earth. She stood, brushed off her hands, gathered the candles and gave them to Nathan. While he finished up, I picked up the empty carton of salt and tugged my athame free from the ground. I wiped it off on my rain-soaked jeans and put it back in the sheath at my waist.

I slid the backpack over my shoulder, took Nathan's hand, looped my other arm through Cy's and grinned at them. "We kicked ass."

"You did," Cypress corrected.

"Told you, you could do it," Nathan said to me.

"I could really use a beer," Cypress said seriously.

"Well sure," I said, and felt a silly grin form on my face. "Save the campus from the malevolent ghost of the school's founder, and we didn't get maimed or killed... I say we deserve to party."

Cypress and Nathan laughed at that, and we walked away from the cemetery.

We'd only traveled a few yards when I kicked something in the grass. Curious, I stopped and bent over to pick it up.

It was one perfect yellow apple.

"Where'd that come from?" Cypress asked. "There aren't any apple trees around here."

"I don't think it came from a tree," I said carefully. "I think it's a thank you gift, and maybe a reminder from Prudence."

"A reminder?" Cypress asked.

"Yeah," I said, tucking the apple in my jacket

pocket. "It's a reminder that we still have something left to take care of."

"She wants her name restored," Nathan said, as we stood in the thinning rain. "She wants her story told."

"We'll find a way," I said, pulling both Cypress and Nathan closer. "The Witches of William's Ford stand together."

EPILOGUE

In the days that followed, the damage to the Harris/Crowly family plot was blamed on the thunderstorm. The general consensus was that the tree that had fallen was previously damaged from September's tornado, thus making it vulnerable to storm winds. The chip off the corner of Victoria Crowly's pink headstone was re-attached, and the fence was repaired and put back into place.

Samhain came and went. Nathan celebrated with the family at the manor. I think he got a real kick out of seeing all of the neighborhood kids trick-or-treating. I know I enjoyed it. As of Samhain night, Nathan and I were officially dating. — I still haven't seen his tattoo. But there's plenty of time for that. I have a hunch when I do... it will be worth the wait.

Construction was restarted on the museum expansion. Since the foundation of the cottage was not classified as being historically significant; it was documented, but eventually filled in and built over.

The suits on the University Board of Governors met and actually decided to do the right thing. Dr. Wallis and Dr. Meyer were instrumental in influencing the final decision. They'd each spoken to the board, proposing that Prudence Thornton and her land were important parts of the campus history, and therefore deserved to be acknowledged. I'd also heard from Bran that the Doctors threatened to contact the local media if the Board of Governors were unreasonable.

Finally it all came down to a vote, and in an interesting turn of events, it was Thomas Drake who tipped the vote over to our side.

So it took a few more weeks, but Prudence's remains were finally laid to rest. In a pretty spot at the far western edge of where the Thornton property had once been, a gravesite was selected. The Witches of William's Ford pitched in and purchased a modest granite headstone. The stone simply read: Prudence Thornton. Born 1849- Died 1878. Midwife and Wise Woman.

The board members of the local history museum led by Dr. Meyers, and the Drake family, took it a step further. They held a fundraiser, arranging for an ornate iron fence to be built around the gravesite and a historical marker to be added to denote where the Thornton property and orchard had once stood.

On a sunny and mild morning in late November, Nathan and I visited the gravesite and planted a pair of small apple trees on either side of the fenced area. After we finished, the two of us joined hands and blessed the new trees so they would flourish and grow strong and true.

I knew that Prudence would have approved.

***

Turn the page for a preview of *Under The Holly Moon*.

Book Five in the Legacy Of Magick series!

Under The Holly Moon

I stood on the front porch of the manor, my suitcases at my side. The Yuletide decorations were up, and the holiday lights glowed in bright festive colors across the porch railings. A huge fresh pine wreath hung on the front door as if to say 'welcome'. I started to open the door, and thought better of it.

I hadn't been home in over two years. Would I even be welcomed?

I'd probably forfeited the right to just waltz back in to the family's house as if only a few days had passed since I'd last been home. I stalled, and called myself a coward. I could see my own reflection in the stain glass of the manor door. My eyes looked tired, my face was pale, and my hair was— as usual— sticking up all over the place. I brushed an annoying curl away from my eyes and tried to smooth my long hair back into place. I took a deep breath and told myself to be brave. The air was sharp and clear, and my breath made little white clouds against it.

While I stood shivering in my pale blue coat, I gathered my courage. Packing and loading up my car on my own and the four hour drive had been *easy* compared to what I was about to do. I'd rehearsed this reunion scene in my mind over and over as I'd driven east. Off to my right a pretty, waxing crescent moon was hanging low in the western sky. That was a good sign. A waxing crescent. A symbol for new beginnings, abundance— and also our family's magickal crest.

I didn't hazard a guess at what my family's reaction would be to my surprise visit... Though actually this wasn't a *visit* at all. Because I hadn't told anyone— not even my family— that I was moving back home. Permanently.

Behind me, parked in the long driveway, my car was stuffed full of boxes, books, clothes, and everything that I'd owned for the past two and a half years while away at school. But instead of returning to Kansas City in January, I hoped to live at the manor and drive across town to class... That was my master plan, anyway. I had transferred to William's Ford University. My schedule was set and there was no going back now.

On an academic level, it could all work out perfectly. That is, if the family took me back in. There was a good chance they wouldn't even welcome me back.

Not after the way I'd acted.

Not after the way I'd treated them.

Not after everything that I'd done.

I had run. Using the convenient excuse of a partial

scholarship to a university clear across state. I had tried to live a mundane life, and swore to put all magick behind me. At the time, escaping William's Ford had seemed to me like my best option.

But I had gone overboard in my attempts to remove any temptation to practice magick. I'd ruthlessly cut off any and all attempts of contact the family had made. I took extra summer classes, visited my father and stepmother in Iowa, or claimed I was simply too busy working to come home on semester or holiday breaks.

Now I was back, and standing on the front porch of the house I'd grown up in made me realize how badly I had missed them all.

I squared my shoulders, reached out, and knocked briskly on the front door. It seemed like forever until it opened. When it did, I found myself face-to-face with my twin sister, Ivy. She wore a long, loosely knit deep green sweater layered over a black gauzy skirt. Leggings and boots completed her outfit, and it was sort of Forrest Witch meets gothic faery tale.

Her hair appeared to be its natural brown color and was cut in a cute, long bob. The front angled sharply to her collar bones while the back was shorter. Her makeup was still dramatic, but yet more subdued then I'd ever seen it. I blinked in shocked surprise

"Ivy? You look so different," I said, and then cringed at how that sounded to my own ears. *What did you expect?* My inner monologue chastised. *You haven't seen her in person for two years.*

"Well, well." Ivy looked me slowly up and down. "If it isn't Holly Irene Bishop. My twin sister who turned her back on her family, and gave up Witchcraft."

"Hello, Ivy," I said, trying a smile.

Ivy leaned against the door jam and stared. "So, how'd that all work out for you?" she said, crossing her arms over her chest and staying within the wards of the house.

"It sucked, actually," I heard myself say.

Ivy raised an eyebrow at me. "It was your choice to stay away. No one made you abjure the Craft." Ivy stopped herself and took a shaky breath. She looked down at my suitcases. "Why are you here now, Holly?"

"I wanted to surprise everyone with a visit for the holidays," I said, bracing myself against the distrust that was written all over her face.

Ivy's green eyes narrowed at me. She glanced significantly towards my car, and shifted her eyes back to mine. "Your car is awfully full for a holiday *visit*. Isn't it?"

Before I could answer, I saw movement in the foyer behind Ivy.

"Jeez Ivy." I could hear my cousin, Autumn. "You're letting all the cold air in," she said as she came into view, wearing jeans and a hot pink sweater. She stopped suddenly and stood staring at me open mouthed. "Holly?"

"Autumn—" was all I managed to say before she was leaping out of the front door and grabbing me up in a hug. My heart jerked once, then settled.

"You're here!" Autumn said, pressing her face along mine. "I had the weirdest dream last night, about seeing a holly shrub and an ivy vine growing up the Yule tree in the foyer." She squeezed me tight, then pulled back and looked deep in my eyes. "Now it makes sense! You're home for good. Aren't you?" she said.

I nodded. "Score another one for the Seer," I said, hugging her back.

"Oh, we've missed you!" Autumn let me go, and grabbed a suitcase. "Come in! Come in." She beckoned me with one hand while she wheeled one suitcase in with the other.

"I wanted to tell you myself..." I laughed and picked up the second suitcase and crossed the threshold. I glanced up at the ward over the front door. To my relief the house didn't reject me.

Autumn shut the door behind us and Ivy stepped back. Before I could begin to try and apologize, or even say anything meaningful to my twin, a small red-haired tornado blew through the foyer.

"My Ivy!" Morgan ran straight to Ivy.

Ivy scooped him up and planted a loud kiss on his cheek. As the little boy laughed, Ivy hitched him on her hip.

Now it was my turn to stare. The last time I'd seen my nephew in person he'd only been a baby. "Hi Morgan."

"Who's that?" he asked Ivy, pointing at me.

Autumn ran a hand over the toddler's head. "It's your Aunt Holly," she said.

"No." Morgan shook his head and frowned at me.

It gave me a jolt to see that my pajama-clad nephew had the same color hair and curls that I did. As I watched, he tucked his head on Ivy's shoulder and I found myself regarded by two very suspicious sets of eyes. One baby blue, the other a sharp green.

While Autumn called for the rest of the family, I watched as my sister and my nephew moved back and farther away from me. Even as Bran, Lexie, and Great Aunt Faye came pouring into the foyer with smiles and welcoming hugs, I willed myself not to cry.

I could feel my sister's hurt and distrust from where I stood. I had no illusions that our relationship would be mended quickly or easily. I had more apologizing and making amends to do to with my twin— than I did with anyone else.

I was back in William's Ford. For better or worse I was home and here to stay. I could only hope that with a little luck and maybe even some magick, I could begin to make things right again.

Under The Holly Moon. Coming December 2016!

Made in United States
Troutdale, OR
07/02/2025

32615943R00156